HURON COUNTY LIBRARY

Clinton
Branch

Date Due

SO-AET-322

JAN 11 '97	JUL 1 2 2004		
FEB 0 3 1997			
DEC 2 1 1998			

4938

J
FIC
Nelso

Nelson, Rosemary, 1946-
 The golden grasshopper / by Rosemary Nelson.
--Toronto : Napolean Publishing, c1996.
 117 p.

798547   ISBN:0929141504 (pbk.)

1. Science fiction. I. Title

DISCARDED

1439   96NOV29   3559/cl   1-447892

THE GOLDEN GRASSHOPPER

by Rosemary Nelson

Napoleon Publishing

DEC 1 0 '96

Text © 1996 Rosemary Nelson

All rights reserved. No part of this publication may be reproduced, stored in a retrieval system or transmitted, in any form or by any means, electronic, mechanical, photocopying, recording or otherwise, without the prior consent of the publisher.

Cover illustration and grasshopper logo: Scott Chantler
Book design: Craig McConnell

Published by Napoleon Publishing,
Toronto, Ontario, Canada

Printed in Canada

05 04 03 02 01 00 99 98 97 96   5 4 3 2 1

Canadian Cataloguing in Publication Data

Nelson, Rosemary, 1946-
        The Golden Grasshopper
ISBN 0-929141-50-4

I. Title.

PS8577.E39G65 1996   jC813'.54   C96-931546-5
PZ7.N45Go 1996

For Dad, with much love and appreciation,
for giving me many "golden grasshoppers."

CHAPTER 1

A fly buzzed slowly around the room and landed on the teacher's bald head.

Why do lazy flies land on a person anyway? Perhaps they're looking for a place to stop and wash their face, or maybe they just want to crawl around and explore. What would there be to explore on a bald head? Would a hungry fly find something to eat on a bald head?

Maybe it had to go to the bathroom!

I covered my mouth so I wouldn't laugh out loud and looked out the window. Fluffy white clouds sailed through an ocean of blue sky. Another perfect Okanagan day and here I was stuck in another boring science class!

I glanced over at my cousin, Paul. Although he's almost a year younger than me, we're both in the same grade. He looked kind of bored too, but he can afford to be. His marks in science are high. I keep getting D's in science on my report card, and my mother's told me that if I don't bring up my science mark this last term of grade five, I'm going to have a tutor over the summer or go to summer school – whichever can be arranged. Yuk! She's been so crabby since my dad left that she just might do it, too.

I think my teacher, Mr. Thomas, has almost given up on me. He's told my mother that I never seem to be listening in science class. He's right. I don't. It's a wonderful time to just let your mind wander. Besides, who wants to learn about things like animals by listening about them, reading about them, and then writing notes.

I know a lot about animals from living with them on a farm. I even know how a cow has a calf. I saw our cow, Pansy, do it last spring. I've also done some experimenting on my own to learn about animals. Well, nearly on my own – I usually make sure that Paul is involved too, so that all the blame won't fall on me if something goes wrong.

A while ago I decided to make a collection of animal footprints in cement. I started with my dog, Roper. Although the prints turned out not too badly, I'd have to say that the experiment was a failure. When Mom opened the door, Roper pulled away from Paul. He leapt out of the grey, gooey mess, past Mom and into the house. It was easy to follow him because of the prints, but it wasn't so easy to catch him. By the time we did, my mother said there would be no more collecting of footprints!

Last summer I brought home a baby skunk after its mother got run over by a car on our road. I planned to observe it and write a book on skunk raising. I would have learned a lot about skunks if Paul hadn't forgotten to close the barn door one night a few weeks later. While we were eating supper Roper must have followed his nose to the barn and surprised the skunk, who by this time was old enough to spray.

The smell was ghastly! We had to move the cows out for two weeks, Roper had to be bathed in tomato juice, and the skunk had to go to the animal shelter. I guess that experiment would also have to be called a failure.

Another thing that bores me in science is reading about stars and planets. Who cares about some old star that's a zillion miles away? Last week I saw a flying saucer, late at night, from my bedroom window. I know I did! If I could have been inside that spaceship, just think what I'd have learned about the stars.

Bottomless black holes and planets with bright haloes around them danced in my head as I dreamed about space.

"And the first prize will be a fully paid trip to Vancouver to visit the Science Centre and the Planetarium." Mr. Thomas's voice cut through the fog of my thoughts. I sat up straight and blinked. It was hard to come back to Earth. I focused on Mr. Thomas's head and noticed the fly was gone. It must have found Mr. Thomas boring, too.

Everyone around me looked excited. My cousin, Paul, was waving to get my attention. Curious, I put my hand up.

"I'm sorry, could you please repeat that?"

Mr. Thomas smiled at me. "Ahh Lisa, I finally have your attention. I'm glad you've decided to join us. For the last ten minutes I've been telling the class about the science fair next month. All entries will be judged and first prize for the best project will be a fully paid trip to Vancouver . . ." I silently mouthed the last words as he said them; ". . . to visit the Science Centre and the Planetarium."

WOW! That's the kind of science I was interested in! Although we live in the Okanagan valley, I'd only been to Vancouver once to visit a sick relative with my parents. But I'd heard all about the Science Centre and the Planetarium. Both sounded like great fun.

Besides, if I won that contest, surely it would bring up my science mark for this last term, and I would be able to have my summer to myself.

Somehow, I HAD to win first prize in that science contest!

CHAPTER 2

Y ou did not, Lisa!"
"I did so. I saw one last week I tell you!"

"You NEVER saw a flying saucer, and I think it's a dumb idea to be out here hoping to get a picture of a spaceship for the science fair. Besides, my dad says there's no such thing!"

I couldn't see Paul's face in the dark. But I just knew how he was standing there with his hands on his hips and his chin stuck out at me. Sometimes he can sure make me mad!

My voice rose. "Well, your dad's stupid, and besides that, he's a liar. I saw one I tell you, and it scared me half to death."

"My dad is not a liar . . . liver lips!" Paul yelled back. "Just because your dad lied before he left doesn't mean my dad tells lies, too."

I don't know which stung more, his calling me "liver lips" or the comment about my dad. I took a step towards Paul. I was going to hit him right where it hurts the most. But my big toe caught in the sleeping bag and I tripped. I fell hard against him and we both crashed to the ground. Roper leapt out of the way.

I heard Paul go "OOMPH" as I landed on top of him. He must have thought I was attacking him. There was a vicious yank on my braid, and then we rolled off the tangled sleeping bag and into the pile of food we'd just spread out for our snack: peanut butter and jelly sandwiches, bananas, and nice thick slabs of chocolate layer cake.

As well as being nearly a year older than Paul, I'm also a whole lot taller. Both of these facts really bug Paul. Sometimes I feel too tall around him, but I was glad at this moment that I was bigger because he was tough for a runt, and I really didn't want to lose this fight.

I felt a sticky wetness begin to ooze through the back of my nightie as we twisted and rolled back and forth over the gooey mess of squashed food. I put my hand up to grab Paul's ear and instead came away with a handful of leaves and peanut butter and jelly.

It suddenly occurred to me how funny we both must look. Laughter began to bubble up from my stomach. I tried to choke it back, but a weird noise escaped from my throat. Paul must have thought I was going to throw up in his face. He pulled away quickly. I sat up and wiped a glob of squashed banana off my arm. A giggle escaped and I collapsed once again onto the mess of food and laughed and laughed until I got the hiccups. Paul was probably staring at me in amazement. He hadn't heard me laugh like that for a long time.

Suddenly a beam of light swung across the lawn and trapped us within its circle. Roper let out a "Woof" as he recognized my mother.

"So that's what the noise was all about – a scrap – and aren't you two a fine looking mess! Well, you'd better come in the house to clean up and then get right to sleep. Seven o'clock comes early."

Paul and I scrambled to our feet. I felt a little guilty. It was only about a half hour ago that Mom had tucked us into our sleeping bags out under a big apple tree in the back of our farmyard. I hadn't told her the real reason why we wanted to sleep out – in fact I hadn't told her about the science fair yet. We just pretended it would be a special treat, and in a way it was. Paul doesn't get to stay out at our farm very often. Mom has been too busy this spring to have company. Too busy and too grouchy!

I stared thoughtfully at the circle of light as I gathered up what was needed to take back to the house. She seemed different tonight. She didn't seem very mad at us. Usually she yells when something goes wrong. We've had some terrible rows in the year since my dad left.

Paul and I trailed back to the house along behind Mom's path of light. Above us winked millions of glittering stars. The sweet strong scent of willows drifted along on the evening breeze. I sighed. The night was really too beautiful to ruin with a dumb fight.

Maybe Paul can't help being a nerd sometimes, or his dad either. I knew what I'd seen last week and nobody was going to change that in my mind. For some reason, I felt pretty sure that the flying saucer would come back and I would be able to get a picture of it, if only Paul would cooperate.

Later, we lay in our sleeping bags in clean clothes and on top of a fresh pile of leaves we'd gathered. Warm May evening breezes rustled the trees above us and played across our faces. A choir of insects sang a midnight serenade which should have lulled us to sleep, but kept me wide awake.

Paul was awfully quiet. He was either asleep or else he was feeling guilty for having been in a fight with me. He'd been told by his mother not to cause Aunt Kay any trouble this weekend, and even though Mom hadn't really been mad, he was probably feeling bad.

"Every time I get into trouble it's because of you," he blurted out in the darkness.

"It is not," I retorted.

"It is so. Remember last year when you decided that we should cook eggs in our microwave for lunch?"

"Well, how was I supposed to know that you have to take the shell off? We don't have a microwave, remember?" I hissed.

"They exploded into a zillion pieces. My mom's still picking eggshell out of it," Paul went on. "It's a good thing she never found out that you tried to talk me into drying our cat in the microwave when she fell in the fish tank."

"That was when I was younger and didn't know any better. Besides, she didn't really fall in. I wanted to see how the fish would react to her, and when I held her over top, she scratched me so I *dropped* her in."

"She ate my piranha," Paul said angrily. "It cost me two weeks allowance."

"Well, which would have been worse? The piranha could have eaten her. They're man-eaters you know." I chuckled to myself. "They're probably cat-eaters, too."

Paul didn't laugh. "And then there was the time you stuck a whoopie cushion on the teacher's chair. You said it was something to do with our science unit on air pressure, but it got us in a lot of trouble . . ."

"Oh, never mind," I interrupted. "You just don't appreciate good ideas for experiments."

"Good ideas! You're always trying to do crazy things that will cause a sensation. I may be younger, but at least I'm not as dumb as you are. I don't even know why I agreed to come tonight. Your goofy idea about getting a picture of a space ship for the science fair is the craziest I've heard."

I decided to ignore him and watch the stars. One bright pinpoint of light in particular seemed to be winking down at me. I stared at it until I felt my eyes closing. I shook my head and once again glued my eyes to the light, which appeared to be slightly bigger and brighter than before. I was beginning to feel it was sending me a message. To keep awake, I tried to concentrate on the soft sounds around us in the dark: trilling, rustling, whispering, crackling.

Paul suddenly sat up. "Lisa, what's that noise?" At this point I was too tired to care. I rolled over so my back was to Paul. "It's probably a Tilywonkin bird," I muttered.

"What's a Tilywonkin bird?" Paul asked. "I've never heard of such a thing."

"Oh yeah? Well, it's actually a long lost distant cousin of Ogopogo, our Lake Okanagan monster." I rolled onto my back and folded my arms at the back of my head. "It's a humongous bird that can't fly. It has a gross, ugly reptilian head and wicked, beady eyes."

Paul was holding his breath beside me. I loved to scare him by telling him silly things. This was almost too much for him to swallow, though.

"What does it eat?" Paul asked in that smarty pants "gotcha" tone.

"It crawls through the underbrush looking for boys who smell like peanut butter. Now go to sleep!" Paul snorted and then was quiet. I shut my eyes and must have drifted off to sleep.

CHAPTER 3

I don't know how long the light had been shining on us, or how long Paul had been rigid with terror beside me before he reached over to tug at my arm.

"Lisa," he whispered hoarsely. "Wake up. Wake up, Lisa!" The tugging became more insistent.

I didn't want to wake up. It felt like I'd just gone to sleep. When I heard Roper whine uneasily, I squinted one eye open.

The area around us was bathed in a harsh, throbbing white light. The grass, now damp with dew, sparkled with dancing silver lights. An eerie high pitched hum hurt my ears. Ahead of us on the grass was the source of the blinding light and weird sound, but everything was so bright I couldn't make out what it was.

I sat up to have a better look. Paul was already sitting, staring with huge eyes at the pulsating light ahead of us. As I shielded my eyes I noticed that the hairs on my arm were all standing at attention.

"Mom?" I called out weakly. Perhaps she was playing a joke on us.

"It's not your mom, dummy," Paul squeaked out of the side of his mouth.

"Well, it's not a Tilywonkin bird either, so what is it?" I muttered back.

I unzipped my sleeping bag. I was going to find out what was going on. Not Paul, though! He had pulled his sleeping bag up around him like a cocoon so that only his nose and enormous eyes could be seen peeping out. With a "yip", Roper headed towards the house with his tail between his legs.

Suddenly, the strange noise stopped and the bright light began to fade. Silence crept in, heavy and thick as if a blanket had suddenly been thrown over the area. There was no more trilling or rustling or whispering or crackling. Everything seemed to be waiting. I pulled the sleeping bag back up and let the darkness sift down around me. The air still felt charged with an energy of some kind that made my body tingle.

All at once a trail of light droplets bounced in an arc through the darkness towards us and then over our heads. Twigs snapped above me and I heard a muffled "Oomph," followed by a string of angry sounds which made no sense at all. I held my breath as I stared at the spot above my head. Suddenly the full moon scuttled out from behind a cloud and moonlight flooded the yard.

Swinging upside down on a lower limb of the tree, trying frantically to right itself, was the strangest creature I'd ever seen. It had very short legs, a large bald head and enormous, unblinking black eyes. Tangled wires led from what appeared to be ears, along its arms and legs to a little box attached to its waist with a belt. Rings of coloured lights raced around the belt.

The angry sounds continued as the creature untangled the wires. Finally, with an embarrassed look, it stood upright on the limb for a second, then jumped off and floated to the ground a few feet away from us.

No use being too brave I decided as I quickly pulled the sleeping bag up over my head and held it tight. Whatever was happening, I didn't want to be a part of it.

"Come out, come out," a musical voice pleaded. "I am not here to hurt you."

I risked making a tiny tunnel in my sleeping bag to sneak a look out. The creature stood staring at me.

"Come out. I will not hurt you," the voice chimed again. It sounded like a machine.

I'd almost forgotten Paul. I turned my tunnel

towards him to find his eyeball peering at me through a tunnel he'd made from his own sleeping bag. I let out a startled shriek.

"Lisa," he whispered frantically, "do something."

"Do something!" I squeaked. "*You* do something!"

"I have already," he moaned. "I just peed my pants." I began to giggle, even though I knew I shouldn't. Paul has this problem. Even though he's in grade five and fairly normal otherwise, he has a weak bladder. When he gets overexcited, he sometimes just can't hold it. I know about it because I'm his cousin, but I've been warned by his mother and my mother *not* to tease him, and *never* to tell anyone else about it.

A tinkling laugh seemed to come from the creature. It stood with its eyes closed, shaking silently, the sound coming from the box around its middle. It no longer seemed so scary. Feeling brave, I pushed the sleeping bag back and sat up.

"Who are you?" I asked in an almost normal voice.

The eyes flew open. "My name is Gagar. Gagar from the planet Ylepithon."

My gaze travelled beyond him to the spot where we'd first seen the blinding light. A small, saucer shaped contraption sat shining in the moonlight, casting eerie shadows onto the surrounding grass.

Gagar! Ha! Fat chance! Sure, I had seen a flying saucer last week up in the sky far away. This one was sitting in my back yard. And even though I'd dragged Paul out to wait for this very thing, I suddenly couldn't believe it. Someone had to be playing a trick.

I could play this silly little game, too. I stood up and faced the creature. "What is your mission here on Earth?" I was sure that's what I'd heard once on a T.V. show. Anyway, it sounded cool.

"My mission here on Earth is to gather fleas. That is why I have come to you," the voice blipped out in musical monotones.

"TO GATHER FLEAS!" I exclaimed. "Come on out, Paul. This guy is harmless. He's just nuts! This has to be some kind of joke."

Silence. I turned to the lumpy sleeping bag at my feet. "Come on out, will ya? Don't be a chicken."

"No, I can't come out. I told you, I wet my pants," he moaned.

"I promise not to look," I said as I crossed my heart and hoped to die.

Paul threw back the sleeping bag and slowly crawled out. He really had wet his pants.

Gagar had taken a step forward and now he

sat with legs crossed, waiting patiently. "Please sit down and I will explain everything."

Paul and I looked down at him. He was very serious. I looked at Paul and shrugged. Then I sat down facing Gagar, and Paul did the same.

CHAPTER 4

M any millenniums ago we lived here on earth," Gagar began. "When the ice ages came, our ancestors had the technology to leave, and they did so. In those years, we looked much different. We had powerful wings that allowed us to fly everywhere. But television and computer technology made us very lazy, and after thousands of years of sitting instead of flying, we began to lose our wings. This is all we have left."

Gagar leaned forward to show us a little knob-like growth on each shoulder which fluttered weakly as he spoke. "And so, a long time ago we developed a way of using flea power to help us fly."

Paul and I both leaned forward and said together, "Flea power to help you fly?"

Gagar nodded his big, solemn head. "You may not realize it, but your common flea is a very powerful insect. He can leap a hundred times his own height. When you put many of them together, you get an incredible store of energy."

Strange noises came out when Gagar opened his mouth to speak again. The lights on his belt blinked on and off. He looked down and gave the little box a good whack. The lights began to race in circles around him again.

"I'm sorry, my translator box is, as you say, 'acting up'. It's not used to running into trees. My unit must be running very low on F.P." He fumbled with the small box again, taking out something from a little compartment on the side.

We strained to see the glowing object he held in his hand, but he jumped up on his tiny legs and stood still for a moment with his eyes closed. Then, to our astonishment, he silently rose into the air, floated over to the tree he had been tangled up in before, and gracefully landed on a limb where he sat looking down at us.

Paul jumped to his feet. "This has to be a dream," he whispered in a daze. "Lisa, pinch me. I want to see if I'm asleep."

What an invitation! I leaned over and pinched him on the backside. He yelped.

"See," I said, smiling at him. "It's not a dream!"

"Children, children, I do not have time to waste," said Gagar, drifting down to us. "The ionospheric conditions will change soon, and before they do, I must be gone."

He stretched his arm out to us and opened his

hand. "This is my flea capacitor. It converts the F.P., or flea power, into energy that allows us to fly. The problem is that our flea colonies on Ylepithon are being wiped out by a contagious virus, so I have come back to Earth to ask you to collect some fleas which will be virus-free. Then we can build up healthy colonies again on Ylepithon."

I must have been staring at him as if I thought he was loony. "Here, try it if you don't believe me," Gagar's voice chimed. He held the flea capacitor out to me.

I stared at the glowing object with dismay. It looked for all the world like a grasshopper. A golden grasshopper. I hate grasshoppers! Even though there are lots of them around the farm every summer, I usually manage to keep out of their way. I hate the way they cling to you with their claws and stare at you with beady, little black eyes and then spit "tobacco juice" on you. YUK!

"Why does it look like a grasshopper?" I asked, trying to keep revulsion out of my voice.

Gagar's monotone chime rose a level with excitement. "Earth's grasshopper is the 'great granddaddy' of jumpers! Can you imagine the store of energy we would get if we could convert their jumping power? But alas, they never survive the journey to Ylepithon. They shrivel up and die."

He sighed. "So as a tribute to that power we use the symbol of the golden grasshopper for our flea capacitor."

I turned to Paul. "You try it."

He stepped backward. "Me? You're the one who's always dreaming about flying. You try it."

That's another thing about Paul I'd almost forgotten. He's afraid of heights. He probably wouldn't admit it, but I remember the day he followed me out my bedroom window and onto the roof to check a bird's nest in the eaves. Suddenly his eyes got big and he turned sort of green looking. He had to crawl back on his hands and knees.

Paul didn't know I hate grasshoppers and I didn't want him to find out I was afraid of anything. He was watching me closely. Perhaps he suspected.

"Oh yeah?" I said. "This silly old grasshopper will let me fly, eh?" Suppressing a shudder, I gingerly picked up the object between my thumb and forefinger.

"You must think about wanting to fly," Gagar said. "This allows the capacitor to work effectively. Now hold it tightly and stroke its back gently."

It felt like a grasshopper, too. It was all I could

do not to fling it out of my hand with a screech, the way I usually do when one lands on me.

Paul had a smirk on his face as he watched me. I closed my eyes and willed my thumb to stroke the horrid grasshopper-like thing. It was easy to think about wanting to fly. As Paul said, lots of nights I dream about flying. I'm always able to leap up into the air and fly away from any danger I want to escape. Other times, I just fly in my dreams for the pleasure of it. Oh, to be really able to fly!

Suddenly, there was no ground under my feet. Effortlessly, my body began to sweep upwards. My eyes flew open and broke my concentration. I collapsed in a heap on the ground a few feet away and sat there dazed.

"Good, good," Gagar said jumping up and down. "That's excellent for your first try. It takes practise to become good at it. Try it again."

I did. This time I knew I could do it if I really tried. Gripping and stroking the golden grasshopper, I concentrated fiercely on wishing to fly, and when I felt myself leaving the ground, I made myself relax.

I rose into the air. The sensation was marvellous. I opened my eyes to look around. A tree nearby put out welcome boughs. I decided to head for it and rest. No sense going too far on one's first flight.

As I sailed over Paul's head, to my horror, he sang out in a loud voice, "I . . . can . . . see . . . your . . . underpants!"

I had forgotten that I really wasn't dressed for flying. With wildly thrashing legs, concentration shattered once again, I smacked into the trunk of the tree, leaving some of the skin from my arms and legs behind as I slithered down it.

I lay still in a crumpled heap till the stars in my head cleared. A second later, Paul's face loomed above me. "They're pink with little blue flowers on them."

"Are you hurt?" he asked as an afterthought.

"You worm," I hollered as I jumped up. "No, I'm not hurt, and if you tell anyone about my underwear, I'll . . . I'll tell them about your PROBLEM."

Paul's hands shot out to cover himself. He'd forgotten what had happened to him earlier. His face drained of colour and I knew that he wouldn't be telling anybody.

Gagar shook his head at us. "Children, children, please pay attention. I must soon be away!" He handed me a small glass bottle. "This must be filled with fleas until the lid glows red." he said. "They will be kept healthy within the interior of this bottle. The red glow will indicate the minimum amount we need to start our new colonies."

I felt my mouth drop open. "You're kidding! Where are we supposed to find that many fleas?"

Gagar shrugged. "The Earth is practically covered with fleas. At least, it was when we lived here. I have other missions to complete in the universe, but I will return one month from today on my way back home. Until then, you will have the use of the flea capacitor. If you complete the task and are able to supply us with the fleas, we will re-charge the capacitor and leave it with you. It should last you the rest of your life."

"But . . . but, what if we can't?" I stammered.

Gagar's black eyes peered at me. "Can't what?" the musical voice blipped.

I swallowed. "What if we can't get that many fleas in a month?"

"If you are unsuccessful, I will know. Your thoughts will transport themselves to me. It will probably mean another trip back or . . ." He frowned. "It might mean that we would have to go back to the kinds of transportation you have here . . . Oh, the noise and the pollution . . . heaven forbid! I was sure that would have disappeared like the dinosaurs . . ." The lights on Gagar's belt blinked once and then with a groan, his translator box became silent.

A low humming sound began around us. As it rose in pitch, the air once again became charged with some kind of energy. The small saucer-shaped vehicle behind us started to glow softly.

Gagar shrugged his shoulders and then bowed slightly to us. He raised his hand in farewell and before we could say "Yes" or "No" to the idea of flea gathering, he dissolved into the darkness. Seconds later, he and the space ship disappeared in a blaze of blinding light.

Moonlight filtered down upon us through the lacy boughs of the trees as Paul and I returned silently to our sleeping bags. It seemed neither one of us wanted to talk about what had just happened. It was all too strange and we were too tired to think straight.

The last sound I remember as I closed my eyes was hearing Paul mutter, "Yuk, these pyjamas are gross!"

CHAPTER 5

"L isa . . . Paul, it's time to get up," Mom's voice rang out from the house.

Time to get up? I felt I'd just barely gone to sleep. I turned onto my side to look at Paul, but he was already awake, lying with his hands behind his head, thinking hard about something.

I yawned into my pillow, scrunching it up into a ball. Something hard was under the pillow. As my hand closed around it, everything that had happened in the night came flooding back.

I looked at Paul again. He was staring at me. "I had a really weird dream last night," he said.

"Was it about this?" I asked, sitting up and opening up my hand to show him the glowing golden grasshopper.

"You mean it all really happened? Gagar and the flying and . . . " Paul lifted the sleeping bag and looked down at himself. He said no more.

I suddenly remembered the camera by the head of my sleeping bag. "Oh no!" I moaned. "I forgot to take a picture last night! How could I?

Now what am I going to do for the science fair?" Paul just looked at me in shock.

Just then Mom stepped around the lilac bush with a smile on her face. My mom had a smile on her face at seven o'clock in the morning? Something weird *was* going on.

"Come on, sleepyheads," she said. "I told you seven o'clock would come early. Those cows need to be milked right away. Dr. Ferguson will be along shortly to check again on Pansy's barbed wire cut. Let's get them milked before then."

"Who's Dr. Ferguson?" I asked suspiciously. If he was a man, I didn't like the idea of him poking his nose around our place.

"He's our new veterinarian. He seems like a nice fellow." And she turned away before I could make any further comment.

She started to walk back to the house. "Oh, by the way, Lisa," she said as she turned to us again. "Don't leave the cows tethered in one spot for so long. There's a circle of grass over here that's been almost destroyed."

Paul and I looked at each other and scrambled out of our sleeping bags. We ran over to the spot. Sure enough, it was right where Gagar's space ship had been resting. The grass within the circle had been scorched by the space ship. We really had been given the gigantic job of flea gathering.

No longer repulsed, I clasped the grasshopper tightly. I could hardly wait to fly again.

○ ○ ○

"Can I try milking too, Aunt Kay?" Paul asked Mom as we looked at Pansy's wire cut. It didn't look bad enough to me to need checking by a vet.

"Sure you can," Mom said. "Come and sit here by Daisy. She's a quiet one for you to learn on. Lisa, you milk Happy, and I'll do Pansy."

Happy is a cow who was definitely misnamed. She should have been called "Miserable". She balks when you try to lead her. She stamps her feet and swishes her tail when she's being milked. She gives us the most milk of the three though, and that's why we keep her. It's usually my job to milk her because I can handle her.

She turned to gaze at me with mournful eyes as I clipped her tail to the side of the stall.

I love milking. Some kids would probably think it's boring, like doing dishes and making beds. But Mom never has to ask me twice to help her with the milking. I love the fresh hay smell that lingers in the barn, and there's just something special about sitting right underneath a big cow.

With your head against her warm tummy, you

can listen to the rumblings and gurglings inside. You can almost become hypnotized by the rhythm of her chewing her cud and the milk going "Squirt . . . squirt" against the side of the pail as you squeeze and pull, squeeze and pull.

I placed my forehead against the heat of her stomach and took in a nose full of cow smell, which really isn't that unpleasant. Today, this was a good place to think. How were we going to come up with a jar full of fleas, and what was I going to do for the science fair now that I'd forgotten to take the picture of the space ship?

Happy stamped her foot. She doesn't like anyone's forehead on her belly. I sat up to flick her leg and scold her. I glanced at Paul who seemed to be catching right on to milking. He had a big smile plastered on his face.

Our cat, Ginger, prowled into the barn and sat down in the aisle between Paul and me. Opening her mouth, she looked at me expectantly. When I aimed a spray of milk at her she lapped at it furiously. Then she took her paw and washed all the droplets of milk off her ears, eyes, and face. We played the same way every morning and every evening. She loved the warm milk, and my aim was becoming quite accurate.

I heard a car drive into our yard. Mom jumped up so quickly she almost knocked over Paul's pail of milk. "That will be Dr. Ferguson. I"ll be right back." She stepped out into the hazy sunlight and disappeared.

I shot another spray of milk at Ginger while she was busy licking her tail. She leapt into the air when the milk caught her on the side of the head. Then I noticed Paul's back was right in line with the cat. I took careful aim and squeezed hard.

Paul jumped with a startled yelp as the milk soaked his shirt. Without breaking rhythm, I aimed into the pail again. "Squirt . . . squirt, squirt . . . squirt."

"Was that you, Lisa?" Paul turned around with a scowl that I couldn't resist. I quickly took aim again and fired – straight into his face and mouth. Milk splattered everywhere.

I thought he'd be mad, but instead he started laughing and gagging as the warm milk trickled down his face and dripped off his chin. Before I could yell "Stop!" he took aim at me and squeezed. He hadn't had the practise that I'd had aiming at the cat's mouth for the last year. The spray of milk shot across the barn and hit Happy on the back of her leg.

Happy threw up her head in alarm and pulled her tail away from the stall where I'd clipped it. She lashed out with her back leg to send the bucketful of milk splashing in all directions. As I scrambled out of the way, her foot, with a thousand pounds of cow behind it, neatly landed on my own thonged foot.

At that moment, Mom and Dr. Ferguson stepped through the doorway of the barn as I screamed in excruciating pain. Dr. Ferguson reached me first. He scooped me up like a sack of potatoes, wet straw and all, and carried me out of the stall.

"Put me down!" I hollered, beating at him with my fists. "Ow! You're hurting my foot! Let go of me!"

Cool grey eyes glanced down at me, and then he looked over his shoulder. "Kay, grab the door, will you? I'll have a look at her foot in the house."

"No!" I screamed. No veterinarian was going to examine my foot. Especially one who called my mother by her first name. I twisted and kicked him hard with my good foot.

In his surprise, Dr. Ferguson's grip relaxed, and he dropped me. I must have landed on the foot the cow had just stepped on, for another excruciating pain shot through my foot, and waves of nausea and blackness swept over me.

CHAPTER 6

Lisa, it's just a badly bruised foot and a bit of a sprained ankle," Mom said, trying to comfort me. "Dr. Melville says you'll be fine in a day or so."

I was lying on the living room couch with my bandaged ankle and swollen black and blue foot surrounded by ice bags, propped up on pillows.

"Yeah, but does Dr. Melville know that my sprained ankle came as a result of being thrown to the ground? How does she feel about that?"

Mom rolled her eyes upward, then glared at me with her hands on her hips. "Dr. Ferguson did NOT throw you to the ground!"

She sat down to put her arms around me. "I know you have angry feelings about Dad sometimes. I've felt the same way. But we have to stop now. There still are a lot of good people around."

"Well, I'll never like Dr. Ferguson!" I retorted, twisting out of her embrace to face the wall.

The side of the couch sprang back as Mom stood up. She sighed, then spoke softly. "No matter how you feel about the situation, you must apologize to Ted . . . Dr. Ferguson. You cannot go around kicking people."

I swallowed hard. So he had finked on me as well. "My leg must have slipped," I muttered.

"Li . . . sa!" Mom scolded me.

I was cornered. "Okay, okay, I'll apologize," I said, hoping that I would never see him again.

I lay there feeling sorry for myself while Mom fixed us some breakfast. Dr. Ferguson had wisely decided to continue his rounds and Mom had dropped Paul off at his house on the way home from the hospital. This wasn't quite the way I had planned on spending my Saturday.

A wet nose beside the couch filled my hand. I looked into Roper's sympathetic brown eyes. Here at last was someone who would understand what I was feeling. I stroked his silky back. The wet nose pushed out of my hand and came over the side of the couch. A long pink tongue slurped over my face. I threw my arms around his neck and hugged him tightly.

Roper sat down abruptly, his tail thumping against the floor, his nose reaching into the air. Then he lifted his hind leg and scratched furiously at his neck. He scratched and scratched and scratched.

I leaned over to part the fur on his neck.

Three tiny insects glared back at me.

"Mom, Mom!" I screamed. "Come quickly!" There was a clatter in the kitchen as Mom dropped something and rushed to the living room.

"Roper has fleas!" I yelled, sending the ice bags flying as I sat up.

"Lisa, calm down. I know Roper has fleas. It's pretty hard to keep them away when you live on a farm. I'll put Brewer's Yeast on him when I get the time."

"Brewer's yeast? What's that?" I asked.

"It's a powder you buy from a health store. It's supposed to be good for you, but it tastes and smells terrible. When I put it on Roper's fur, the fleas can't stand it so they all leave. It's safer than flea powder, and cheaper. I just haven't got around to doing it lately."

"I'll do it, I'll do it! I want those fleas." Maybe it wouldn't be so hard to collect fleas for Gagar after all. Mom frowned. "Whatever for?"

"We're . . . uh . . . studying them at school this next while," I said, crossing my fingers behind my back so that my white lie would be forgiven. "And . . . and there's a science fair coming up that I'm going to win so my science mark will come up. I'm going to think of a project that will use fleas, so we need a whole bunch," I babbled.

Suddenly, I wondered if I really could think

of a way to use them for my science project. Then, to use one of my mother's favourite expressions, I'd be killing two birds with one stone.

Her frown deepened. "Using those horrible little creatures? Why?"

I gasped. "Well, they're actually very interesting animals. Did you know that they can jump one hundred times their own height?"

"Really," she exclaimed. "Well, that doesn't surprise me. That's how they spread so quickly – ugly little things!" She looked at me again, happy, I'm sure, to see that the black mood I'd been in was gone. "Yes, you can be the deflea-er around here for the next while."

"Mom?" I called as she started back to the kitchen. "Do I really have liver lips?"

"Liver lips! Whoever said that you have liver lips?" she asked, coming back over and looking down at me.

I looked away. "Paul did . . . last night when he was mad at me."

Mom crouched down and took my hands in hers. Her blue eyes twinkled, and a hint of a smile showed at the corners of her mouth. "You have lovely lips that some young man will enjoy kissing some day. In fact, with your auburn hair and blue eyes, you're going to be a beautiful young lady."

"Yuk!" I shrieked. "Kissing . . . Yuk . . . yuk . . . yuk!"

Mom laughed and stood up. "Can you hobble to the kitchen now for breakfast? Here are your crutches."

As I followed her to the kitchen, I stole a glance into the mirror above the dining room table and, to my surprise, saw my reflection pursing its lips at me.

CHAPTER 7

On Monday, Mr. Thomas began a science lesson on how animals protect themselves. I looked at my bandaged foot propped on a chair. I obviously didn't need to listen to this lesson. I know how a cow protects itself from a "dough brain" like Paul. It jumps on top of the nearest person!

I began thinking about the science fair again. What kind of project could I do with the fleas we were to collect? I'd once read that someone had trained fleas to perform a miniature circus act. I wondered how you'd go about teaching a flea to pole vault, or better yet, teach one to ride bareback on a beetle's back.

I daydreamed my way through the rest of the lesson, but just before Mr. Thomas dismissed us, I heard him mention the science fair again, telling us not to wait too long before starting on our projects.

At recess, the playground was buzzing with ideas about the science fair. Everyone in our class was trying for that prize. But nobody needed to win it like I did. For once, I was quiet.

I can think better when I'm upside down and my face is all red from the blood pooling in my brain. I had figured out a way, even with my injured foot, to climb the bar dome and hang upside down with my legs hooked over a bar. That's where I hung now, listening and thinking, my hair falling halfway down to the sawdust on the ground.

Like me, most of the kids still didn't have much of an idea what they were going to do. Michael Black, though, seemed pretty sure of himself and his project.

"Well, what is it if it's so good?" Paul sneered at him.

That's not the way you get the smartest kid in the class to tell you about his project, I thought to myself. Not only is Michael Black smart, he is . . . I hate to admit it . . . also very good looking. There were always girls hanging around him, flirting and hitting him so that he'd chase them. Not me, though. I'd never like any boy enough to chase him.

Michael grinned at his circle of admirers, his blond hair shining in the sunlight. "You think I'm nuts? I'm not going to tell my idea. You'd just copy it. You wait and see. I bet you

I'll win that trip to Vancouver."

At that moment, the bell rang to end recess, and there was a mad rush to line up at the classroom door.

"Hey, look what I found!" a voice yelled as I struggled to grab the bar above me with my arms. When I looked down I spotted the golden grasshopper in the sawdust where it must have fallen from my pocket. Brad Summers, another boy from our class, was about to pick it up.

"That's mine!" I yelled as he scooped it up. "It fell out of my pocket. Give it back, Worm Face!"

"Don't hafta. Finders, keepers . . . losers, weepers," he sang out as he ran out of sight around the corner.

I was in big trouble now. Brad Summers, better known as Worm Face, can be a big pain. He's the type of kid you try to avoid because everything he does bugs you. He goes out of his way to be mean and nasty. What if I was never able to get the golden grasshopper back?

That wasn't the only trouble I was in, though. While I'd figured out a way to hang upside down on the dome, I hadn't thought about getting up again. Every time I tried to swing my arms up, a severe pain would shoot through my leg. I couldn't drop off head first either because my leg hurt too much.

I looked around for help. Everyone had

vanished. Even Paul hadn't noticed that I'd been left behind. It isn't that we're such keeners to get back to class at our school. The fact is that if you aren't back within one minute after bell time, you have a half hour detention after school.

I thrashed about for what seemed an eternity, my face and brain definitely very full of blood. Finally, I began to yell.

Mr. Thomas's frowning face appeared at the window. Then his expression changed. I don't think he believed what he was seeing. Within seconds, he was beneath me helping me down while twenty-five kids had their noses pressed against the window. Brad Summers, with a smirk on his "worm face", was one of them.

"Lisa," Mr. Thomas said with an amused look as we walked back to the school, "please try to stay right side up, until you are off your crutches, at least."

My face and brain were beginning to feel normal again. "Th . . . Thanks, Mr. Thomas. I think I will," I said as I hobbled along beside him.

After recess on Mondays we always have creative writing. While Mr. Thomas is a lousy science teacher, he is excellent at teaching creative writing. He always tries to get us to think about our writing and he has interesting ways of doing it.

Today, he told us we were going to go to the gym for a few minutes before our writing, to "try our wings".

"Try our wings! Don't tell me this is something to do with flying," I thought – not when Worm Face had the golden grasshopper.

It was still in his hand. I could see the tail end of it glowing as we walked down the hall towards the gym. I hopped faster. If I could catch him, I'd nail him with one of my crutches until he gave it to me. He looked over his shoulder and when he saw me coming, he began shoving his way through the line, ignoring the other kids' protests, until he was directly behind Mr. Thomas.

"Sissy!" I snarled at him as I slid onto one of the benches to watch.

"Okay, spread out everyone and find a space where you're away from anyone else," Mr. Thomas shouted. Then, as each kid found a spot and quieted down, he dropped his voice. "I want you to imagine that you are able to fly. It would be a wonderful sensation, wouldn't it? We're going to close our eyes and start moving around the gym clockwise. When I say 'fly', I want you to leap as high as you can into the air and land as softly as you can. Imagine that you are truly airborne."

I gripped my crutches tightly. "Oh no," I moaned. This could be disastrous.

"Okay, let's begin," I heard Mr. Thomas say. The "pitter, patter" of lightly running feet was the only noise to be heard in the gym as the kids pranced around in a big circle.

Paul glided by me. "He's got the grasshopper," I whispered loudly.

Paul's eyes flew open. He looked back over his shoulder at me. "Who has?" he whispered.

"Worm Face has our golden grasshopper," I whispered hoarsely. "Do something."

Paul came to a standstill and glanced at Mr. Thomas, who was standing in the middle of the gym with his eyes closed, and then at Brad Summers, who was jack rabbiting around the opposite side of the gym. He was running too fast, with his eyes squeezed shut and his hands out in front of him. No doubt he was hoping to run into someone and knock them off their feet.

"Fly-y-y!" crooned Mr. Thomas's soothing voice.

We watched, horrified, as twenty-four kids leapt high into the air with smiles on their faces and dreamy visions of flying in their minds. Twenty-three of them landed softly as they'd been instructed. Brad kept going!

He floated past two of the kids and then

bumped hard into a third kid, knocking him to the floor in a tangle of arms and legs. At the same moment, the two kids who'd been coming behind Paul crashed into him and all three of them toppled to the floor. Everyone else collapsed on the floor in fits of laughter.

"Okay, okay, everybody on your feet. Spread out again. Let's try it once more. Have you been into the laughing gas, Brad?" Mr. Thomas asked as he watched Worm Face doubled over in laughter.

Brad was obviously enjoying himself. He was so dumb that he probably hadn't even realized he'd become airborne. Maybe he hadn't concentrated very hard the first time. But next time he might really take off.

"Get ready . . . go," Mr. Thomas called. This time he watched the kids.

"Oh no," I moaned again. Brad was trotting around the gym towards me. I watched as he approached with his eyes closed, making silly faces.

Quickly, I dragged my crutch out from under the bench and shoved it in front of Brad just as I heard Mr. Thomas once again croon, "Fly-y-y!"

And fly Brad did. He soared up into the air, knocking the crutch out of my hand. There was a *twang* as his head hit the basketball hoop above us.

His eyes flashed open. He lost concentration and crashed to the ground on top of my crutch. The golden grasshopper flew from his grasp and I dove off the bench after it.

"Brad!" Mr. Thomas stood wide-eyed above us. "I never knew that you could jump like that! Where have you been hiding during track and field? I expect you to be out at the next practise, my boy – no excuses. You're going to win this school some ribbons!"

Brad stumbled to his feet. "I am?" he muttered rather stupidly. I don't think he'd ever jumped before in his life.

"And Lisa," Mr. Thomas eyed me as I crawled back to the bench. "You seem to be having a great deal of trouble staying on your feet today. Your foot is certainly causing a problem!"

"There's no problem, Mr. Thomas," I said as I gathered my crutches and got in line to go back to the classroom. "No problem at all," I thought to myself with a smile, squeezing the golden grasshopper in my pocket. Now I knew how I was going to win the science fair!

CHAPTER 8

L and P's Flying Machine! Are you nuts?" Paul's loud voice echoed through the barn. "You expect this to fly? It's just a bunch of cardboard boxes taped together." He kicked at it disgustedly.

I clenched my fists. "Don't kick it or it'll fall apart! It's not finished yet. That's where you can help." I took a breath and closed my eyes. "It will too fly. Don't forget, we've got this." I opened my hand to reveal the golden grasshopper.

Paul gasped. "That would be cheating!"

I tossed my head back. "Not really. We still have to make the darn thing work. It's your job to make it look more real. You've made all sorts of model airplanes. You must have some ideas."

Paul peered critically at my flying machine. "I do have one idea. I think we should throw this in the re-cycling bin and start over."

Sometimes cousins can be okay. Within an hour or so, Paul and I had constructed a more likely-looking flying machine. With a hammer and nails and scraps of plywood that we found out behind the barn, we made a platform with wings sprouting off each side. We nailed a wooden crate onto it for a seat. It was only big enough for one person, but Paul said there was no way that he was going on it anyway. At the front we nailed an upright piece of board. Onto this we fastened a propeller which I could turn with a crank from my seat.

We stood back to admire our handiwork. "All it needs is a coat of paint and a sign saying *L and P's Flying Machine*," I said.

Paul looked away. "I think you should make that just *Lisa's Flying Machine*. I don't care about winning that contest anyway."

I turned to face him. "Oh yes, you do. You're just afraid that this is another one of my hair-brained schemes that will get you in trouble. It'll work I tell you."

"Have you even tried the golden grasshopper yet?" Paul asked dubiously.

"No, I just got off my crutches this morning, remember? That's what we're going to do right now, though. Come on."

Paul ran after me as I headed for the house. "Where are we going"?

I looked over my shoulder. "To my room. I don't want anyone to know about this."

On the way upstairs, we passed Mom talking

on the telephone. "I'll see you in about half an hour then," she was saying softly.

I stopped as she hung up. "Who's coming in a half an hour?"

Mom looked me squarely in the eye. "Ted Ferguson's stopping by. It will give you a chance to apologize."

I felt the colour drain from my face. I thought she'd forgotten about that. "How . . . how come he's coming? Pansy's leg is better now."

Mom's face turned a bit pink. "He's not coming to see Pansy. He's coming over to have a cup of coffee with me."

The scent of warm cinnamon buns was in the air. My favourite! Mom hadn't made them for a long time and now I was pretty sure they hadn't been made for me. Suddenly, I felt all funny inside. I turned quickly so that neither Paul nor Mom could see my face and marched upstairs to my bedroom with Paul close behind.

I locked the door behind us and flopped down on the bed. I stared at the figures on the wallpaper above the headboard. Paul watched me for a few minutes without saying anything.

"I don't think he's so bad," he finally said.

"Who?" I growled.

"Dr. Ferguson," Paul replied. "He actually seems kind of nice."

"Kind of nice!" I shrieked. "That's easy for you to say. He's not planning to marry your mother."

Paul hooted. "Who said he wanted to marry your mother? He's only coming over for a cup of coffee!"

I could feel my eyes filling up with tears. "Yeah, but coffee today and before long they'll be going out, and then they'll be talking about getting married. I saw the goofy way they looked at each other the other day. We don't need another man around here." I punched the dresser with my fist and swallowed hard. "Besides, what if he lies to us the way my dad used to?"

Paul was silent. I guess I'd asked him a question that he couldn't answer. "Come on," he suggested, "try the grasshopper. I've got to get home soon."

I brushed my sleeve across my eyes as I retrieved the golden grasshopper from its secret spot in my dresser. The subject of my mother and Ted Ferguson was closed as far as I was concerned. It was clear that Paul didn't share my feelings about the situation, but I couldn't help the way I felt.

I stood in the middle of my bedroom grasping the golden grasshopper in my hand. As I stroked its back with my thumb, I closed my eyes and thought hard about flying. I started to feel funny, weightless – I'd almost forgotten the feeling. Remembering that I mustn't lose my concentration, I opened my eyes to see Paul in the corner beneath me. His fist was jammed in his mouth and his eyes were like saucers. There was at least a metre of space between my feet and the floor.

"Wowee, look at this!" I yelled, kicking my legs and flapping my arms like wings. I rose higher. I put my hands up to prevent hitting the ceiling, forgetting the light fixture which hung behind me in the centre of the room. As I fluttered and bumped along the ceiling like a gigantic moth, a kick from my foot sent it swinging wildly back and forth.

To avoid it, I headed for the tall bookcase which stood beside the door, loaded with books and favourite junk I'd collected over the years. The light fixture's mad flight back and forth must have loosened some screws, because suddenly the glass lamp shade hurtled off like a missile. I had planned to land gracefully on top of the bookcase. Instead, as the glass ball shattered against the wall, I smashed hard against the bookcase.

I watched in horror as it slowly toppled over

into the room with a rumbling crash. Books, dolls, puzzles, jars of bugs and worms, and dried up peanut butter and jam sandwiches hurtled in all directions.

Thinking quickly, I scrambled to unlock the door. Mom doesn't like me locking it and I knew that she'd be here at any moment.

My room looked like a bomb had hit it. I didn't know whether to laugh or cry. As Mom's footsteps pounded up the stairs, I looked at Paul. When the door flew open, we both knew enough to look scared to death and ready to cry.

"We're sorry, it was an accident. There was a big, ugly moth up there in the corner," I babbled before Paul could open his mouth to say something stupid. I shuddered. "You know how I hate moths! So I climbed up on my bookcase to kill it, and it fell over."

Mom looked at everything in dismay. "What happened to the light fixture?"

I held my breath.

"I don't know," Paul suddenly wailed. "It must have kicked it on its way down."

She stepped back and looked down at him. "What must have kicked it?"

Paul looked stricken. "The bookcase. The bookcase must have kicked it."

Mom laughed. "Oh Paul, sometimes you have

such a cute way of saying things."

She hugged us both. "It's okay. I'm glad that neither of you are hurt. Let's get this mess cleaned up. Paul, you run down and get the broom and dustpan for the glass. Lisa, you and I can push this back up and then you can put your things away." She eyed a crust of mouldy peanut butter sandwich. "From the look of things, it was time for some cleaning anyway."

As Mom finished sweeping up the glass, Roper started to bark. A car was turning into the driveway.

"That will be Ted," Mom said, standing up and smoothing her hair with her hands. I suddenly noticed that she was wearing red lipstick and even a touch of eyeshadow. She hadn't done that in ages. It must be getting serious, just as I'd expected.

A wave of guilt flooded over me unexpectedly. I threw my arms around her and hugged her tightly. "Thanks Mom, for not being mad. We're really sorry."

Mom looked surprised for a moment. I don't usually show my feelings that way. As she turned to leave she said, "Don't forget, Lisa, I'd like you to come down in a few minutes and apologize to Dr. Ferguson."

CHAPTER 9

Thinking about the apology made me feel as if a stone were sitting in my stomach. I just knew that I couldn't face Dr. Ferguson. Sometimes I do dumb things when I get mad, and I knew that kicking him that day had been a really dumb thing. Surely if I put if off until another day, at least it would be easier.

"Quick," I whispered to Paul, "help me open the window."

"What for?" Paul asked suspiciously.

" 'Cause I'm going out to try some more flying," I answered. I didn't really know what I was going to do, except escape from the house. I figured that Mom wouldn't spend much time looking for me with Dr. Ferguson around.

"Oh no, you don't," Paul whispered to me angrily. "You're not getting me into any more trouble today."

I snorted. "I didn't get you in any trouble. Mom even thought that dumb thing you said about the bookcase kicking the light fixture was cute. That could have got us in a lot of trouble. Come on, help me open this window. If you do, I'll put everything back on the bookcase myself."

The windows on our old farmhouse were hard to open, but after a lot of straining and tugging, we were finally able to slide the window up high enough so I could crawl onto the sloping red roof.

Paul stared out after me. The look on his face told me he expected another catastrophe at any moment. "I've got to get going. I'll see you tomorrow," he said quickly.

"Wait a minute," I hissed as I hunched down to peer over the edge of the roof. The ground was a long way down!

"Come back, Lisa," Paul pleaded. "You could get hurt."

But I was already airborne. I was getting the hang of this flying business. I stretched out to sail across the roof in front of Paul's white face, just to prove I was in control. Then, with a deep breath, I zoomed over the edge of the roof.

Wow! What a feeling! I soared above the dark velvet lawn below me. A cool breeze swept past my face as I stretched my arms and climbed higher into the air.

"Hi Robin," I yelled, gliding over top of an apple tree and looking down at her nest. I headed for a row of tall poplar trees. "Whooee! Look out, treetops. Here I come!" I zoomed up over the trees, panicking a group of crows meditating in the nearby branches. They didn't stick around but took off in a cawing, flapping mass.

After a couple of sweeps over the garden I practised turning. I felt like Superman! I looked at the fluffy white clouds above and wondered if the golden grasshopper could go that high. Then I remembered Paul. He was watching me from the window, his mouth hanging open. He waved frantically at me.

"Lisa, come back inside!" he croaked as I swept past him triumphantly.

"No way! This is a blast. You've got to try it . . . "

But I had forgotten that Roper was outside. As I sailed out over the side of the house once more, I spotted him wandering along with his nose to the ground. He was obviously on the trail of a buried bone or a cat, either of which make Roper's day.

When my shadow swept over him, he stopped in his tracks to look up. The creature flapping madly above him must have thrown terror into his doggy heart. The fur on his back bristled and his tail whipped between his legs, and with an anguished howl, he raced around to the front of the house. From the protection of the door he went into a frenzy of barking.

Paul's face disappeared from the window. I hovered in the air for a moment, uncertain what to do next. If I landed here, I would be face to face with Mom and Dr. Ferguson who would likely be out soon to investigate Roper's barking. I headed for a tall tree at the edge of the driveway. I managed a graceful landing up near the top where I would be hidden by the leaves.

When Mom and Dr. Ferguson appeared at the corner of the house, Roper was barking crazily at the tree I was hiding in.

I glanced down and gasped. There, far beneath me on the ground, gleaming in the sunlight, lay the golden grasshopper. I must have dropped it when I grabbed hold of the branch I was sitting on.

How could I get down without it? I could climb down a bit further, but then there was a section where the branches were too far apart to reach.

At that moment, Paul, his head scrunched low over the handle bars, went hurtling by on his bike, heading for home. I could tell by the look on his face that there was no use calling for him to stop. What a chicken!

I did some fast thinking. I was not going to be able to clamber down without help. The longer I waited, the worse off I'd be. Besides, Roper was bringing Mom and Dr. Ferguson right to my tree.

I climbed down as far as I could and waited.

Mom stared up at me in disbelief. "Lisa! What on earth are you doing out here? I didn't hear you come downstairs." Dr Ferguson stood behind her with an amused look.

I swallowed hard. "Well, I didn't want to disturb you so I quietly . . . sort of . . . glided down."

Mom shaded her eyes to see me better. "Come down now. You're up too high as it is."

I swallowed again over the lump that stuck in my throat. "I . . . I can't get down," I finally managed to say.

"You can't get down? Well, how did you get up there in the first place?" she asked.

"I . . . I sort of jumped up. And now I can't jump back down. It's too far."

Dr. Ferguson leaned forward to say something to Mom. After a couple of seconds he turned to walk away. My mother would never be able to get me down herself.

"Don't leave me! I'm sorry I kicked you," I blurted out before I could stop myself.

Dr. Ferguson turned back to look up at me with a small smile. His eyes bore into mine for a moment. "Apology accepted, Lisa." He turned away again. "I'll be back in a minute. I'm going to get a ladder."

The ladder itself was no good. It was only long enough to reach the lower branch that I couldn't get down to anyway. I had visions of a dark and lonely night up in the tree by myself. My body ached from the tension. Then Dr. Ferguson was climbing the ladder. Near the top, he braced his knees against the ladder and stretched his arms up.

"Can you reach my hand with your foot?" he asked.

I looked down. Maybe I could if I stretched myself. It looked scary. "I . . . I think so," I whispered.

"Then turn around and back down. Hold onto the trunk for support," he called up.

I did as he said. I grabbed the trunk tightly with both hands. Then I gingerly stretched my left leg down as far as I could, groping for the support of his hand.

I stopped, afraid to leave the security of the limb I was on. Dr. Ferguson felt me hesitate. "Trust me, Lisa. I won't let you fall."

Those words had a familiar ring. My father had said "Trust me" to both my mom and me. Then he had left with another woman. Mom had cried and cried, and I had decided never to trust anyone again when they said "Trust me."

Dr. Ferguson's steady grey eyes made me want

to believe him. At least for the time being. Besides, what choice did I have?

I took a big breath and let my weight sink into his hand as I scrabbled down the trunk. In a few seconds I was able to reach the ladder with my own hands and he, without a word, stepped down the ladder ahead of me.

I was shaking like a leaf by the time I reached the ground. I quickly retrieved the golden grasshopper. Mom had started back to the house and Dr. Ferguson was taking the ladder away from the tree.

I waited for him. This was going to be hard, but it had to be done. I looked at the ground and pushed a leaf around with my toe. "Thank you for helping me down," I said quietly. "I really am sorry about kicking you the other day. It was a dumb thing to do."

Dr. Ferguson looked down at me with a hint of a smile at the corners of his mouth. "Well, Lisa, when you're a veterinarian, you kind of get used to being kicked, or bitten for that matter, although it's usually by four-legged critters." He continued to look at me as a thoughtful frown replaced the smile. "Most often when a critter kicks or bites me, it's because they're afraid that I'm going to hurt them somehow." He paused for a moment. Then as he walked on he said, "I'm not planning on hurting you, Lisa . . . or your mother for that matter."

I stopped and stood still as he walked ahead of me, not seeming to notice. I suddenly felt confused. It was as if he knew and understood what I was feeling. But there was something I had to make clear to him just the same.

"We don't need a man around here. My mom and I can handle things just fine," I shouted at his back.

Dr. Ferguson turned with that irritating smile on his face again. "You'd better stay out of trees that are too tall for you then."

He walked away whistling and I stuck my tongue out at his retreating back. He disappeared inside the house without another glance in my direction.

CHAPTER 10

Paul and I pressed our noses against the cool window, listening to the water drip off of the roof. The yard was a mass of puddles which would be fun to run through later. But right now we had a job to do.

We had decided we'd better start gathering fleas. Time was passing quickly and, as of yet, we didn't have a single flea in the little jar that Gagar had left us. I was pretty sure that my flying machine would allow me to win the science fair, but I wanted to make sure that Gagar would recharge the golden grasshopper so that I would be able to fly for the rest of my life.

"What a fun way to spend a Saturday," Paul moaned, as he continued to stare at the grey world outside the window, "defleaing a dog in a rain storm."

"We're not going to do it out there, silly," I said as I went to the fridge for the Brewer's Yeast. "We're going to do it right here by the fire." Mom had gone into town to shop. Before she left she'd lit the wood stove in the living room to take the chill off the room.

Paul gasped. "In the house? Did your mom say it's okay?"

I headed for the linen closet. "No, I forgot to ask her. She won't mind, though. Besides, we'll be all done and cleaned up by the time she comes home."

I spread one of Mom's white sheets on the carpet in front of the fire. It would be easier to see the fleas on something white. I set down the container of Gagar's, a drinking glass and a piece of paper (which we planned to use to capture them) and a bowl of the soupy mixture of Brewer's Yeast and water I had mixed in the kitchen.

Something was missing. Paul and I looked at each other. "Where's Roper?" we both said together.

Roper has this strange knack for knowing when something concerns him. Whenever it's bath time or time to visit the veterinarian, Roper disappears. The last time we had to take Roper for his shots, we looked everywhere until we finally found him cowering in the laundry basket amongst the dirty clothes.

"That darn dog must be able to read my mind," I muttered as I checked the laundry basket again. He wasn't there – in fact, he wasn't anywhere. We looked through the entire house in all the places a dog might hide. Behind the couch, under the beds, under the table, behind the plant stand and even in the bathroom, although I was sure that he wouldn't be there. The tub was in there and "tub" to Roper meant bath.

We started to think that we'd never find him. I wasn't sure how long Mom would be gone and although I hadn't admitted it to Paul, I didn't really want her to find out that we'd de-fleaed Roper in the house.

As I passed the upstairs linen closet, I thought I heard a noise – almost like a whimper. I opened the door and there, under the bottom shelf, in a nest he'd made from a pile of linen, lay Roper.

Sad eyes looked up at me, and another whimper escaped from his throat. "You're lucky you made a sound," I scolded. "We might never have found you and you might have perished. Last year a mouse died in there you know, Roper. It dried up to nothing," I added for effect.

"Oh, yuk!" exclaimed Paul, his eyes wide. "Didn't it smell?"

"Yeah, it stunk for ages. We finally had to re-paint the closet. I think you can still smell it if you stick your head right in and sniff." I gave

Paul's head a push as if I were going to push him into the closet with the ghost of the dead mouse. He yelped and jumped out of my grasp.

"Come on out. We've wasted enough time," I called to Roper. But he just lay there with his nose on his paws and that unhappy look in his eyes. He wouldn't budge.

The only thing that saved us was the fleas. Roper suddenly got an itch and there just wasn't enough room to scratch, so he "belly crawled" out of the closet and had a good scratch.

No amount of coaxing would get him to follow us downstairs, though. Paul and I finally had to carry him down and deposit him on the white sheet, where he lay quivering and moaning while I applied the gooey mess.

I started up around his neck because that's where I'd seen the fleas. I figured they would move down his body so that by the time I got to the tail area, they would all hop off onto the sheet and we could easily capture them.

"Phew, this stuff stinks. It's gross," Paul muttered as he squatted beside me, holding his nose with one hand and Roper's head down with the other.

"Not only is it gross, it's vile," I said to Paul as I wrinkled up my nose. "Vile" was a new word that we'd learned at school the other day. It meant "wretchedly bad or repulsive". I liked the sound of the word. "Can you imagine people actually eating this stuff?" I went on.

"Yuk!" snorted Paul. "You'd never catch me eating it." For one terrible moment I fought the urge to plant a handful of the stinky mixture on Paul's face. It would be so easy because both his hands were busy. I started to giggle and Paul, not knowing what I was giggling about, started to laugh too.

Although the smell was awful, I was kind of enjoying the feel of the gooey mess as I slathered it onto Roper with my hands. It had run down my arms to my elbows. The three of us must have looked like quite a sight.

Roper had almost given up. He lay in a dis-couraged heap, looking at some faraway object with mournful eyes. Every so often, he groaned.

When I reached Roper's tail, I looked closely. I didn't see any fleas about to leap off onto the white sheet. In fact, I didn't see any fleas at all.

There was just a bit of goo left in the bottom of the bowl. Paul was still sitting holding his nose and Roper's head and laughing. Suddenly I couldn't resist. I scooped up the last handful and before Paul could stop me, I smeared it all over his face.

He jumped up, spluttering and gagging,

uttering words neither one of us are allowed to use. Then, before I could stop laughing and get out of the way, he had taken both hands and scraped off what he could from his face and plopped it on top of my thick, dark red hair. Some of it dribbled down my forehead into one eye. The rest went down the back of my neck.

We stood there leaning against each other in a fit of laughter. Roper thumped his tail on the floor in appreciation. He must have thought it was our turn to be plastered in the smelly mess.

Suddenly the front door opened, and my mother stood in the doorway, bags of groceries in both arms, staring at us with her mouth open.

"Lisa! What on earth is going on?" she said, not too quietly, as the grocery bags slid unnoticed to the floor.

"We were just defleaing Roper, Mom, the way you told us to, with Brewer's Yeast and water," I babbled, looking out of the corner of my eye at Paul. His face looked like he'd just seen a ghost.

"Brewer's Yeast and water!" Mom exclaimed. "I never told you to mix it with water. You just sprinkle the dry powder onto the animal's coat and the fleas leave."

"I didn't see any leave," I muttered.

"Well, you probably drowned them all with that horrible mess," Mom said. "Just look at poor

Roper." She took a step closer. "Lisa," she shrieked, "that's my best linen tablecloth. Get that dog off my tablecloth and bathe him immediately!"

Roper had struggled to his feet, his head hanging, and whining as if asking for sympathy. Then he did what any dog does when he's soaking wet. He hunched over and shook himself hard, sending globs of Brewer's Yeast spewing in all directions. Some hit the wood stove and, with a sizzling sound, burned onto the stove, making a terrible stink!

At that point the word "bath" must have penetrated Roper's foggy brain. He leapt off the table cloth and raced out of the room, spraying wet Brewer's Yeast behind him.

"Catch that dog!" Mom yelled at Paul and me, which didn't make much sense since we'd already made a mad dash after him. We were in big trouble and we knew it.

I couldn't believe how fast Roper could move or how sneaky he was. We would have him cornered and just as we were about to grab him, he would slither between our legs or jump over our arms and race to another part of the house.

By the time we finally caught him and hauled him, yowling and struggling, off to the bathtub, most areas of the house had had the Brewer's

Yeast treatment. Even Mom had flecks of it splat-tered on her jeans and blouse.

○　○　○

It was much, much later that we sat around the kitchen table having a bedtime snack with Mom. We all looked shiny and clean. Roper, with his hair all silky and wavy, once again had a smile on his face. I slipped him a cookie under the table. After all, he had been through a lot today.

Mom had phoned Auntie Teresa to ask if Paul could stay the night. Mom told her she would like Paul's help for some extra work around the place. Auntie Teresa hadn't objected, so we'd bathed Roper, then ourselves. By then the Brewer's Yeast was dry, so Paul and I vacuumed the entire house – carefully – while Mom watched. The stove would have to wait until morning when it had cooled. That was to be our job, too.

"In the meantime," Mom muttered, "the place smells like a brewery. Let's hope no one comes to visit unexpectedly."

Paul and I did not complain. We knew we had gotten off easy. The annoying part was that we'd lost out on all those fleas.

Mom even laughed a little as we sat munching on our cookies. "The next time you two decide to de-flea Roper, let me show you how to do it."

I yawned. I was beat. "That's okay, Mom," I said. "I think Roper's rid of fleas for awhile. Besides, I have another plan for getting some fleas . . . to study at school." Mom's eyebrows went up. I quickly added, "Not here, though – it won't happen here."

As I slurped the last of my milk, I looked at Paul out of the corner of my eye. He had stopped chewing his cookie and was watching me warily.

CHAPTER 11

I had figured out my plan as we'd cleaned the house. Chores always give me time to think. If I have a problem, usually by the time I've finished the job I've also figured out a solution.

We had just over a week left to collect a lot of fleas, and so I figured the more people helping us collect them, the better.

My idea was to ask Mr. Thomas, our science teacher, if we could study fleas as an extension to the animal unit. Then when he said, "Yes" – I wouldn't even consider the possibility of him saying "No" – I would tell the kids how to collect fleas so we could observe them at school.

I chewed on my lip as I considered ways of getting them to give me fleas. Considering what I know about kids, which should be a lot, since I am one, I chose the one that made the most sense to me. All kids love cake and cookies. Paul and I could bake some to trade for fleas during recess.

I thought Paul might call this another wild

scheme and refuse to help, but to my surprise, he didn't. He did wonder, though, where we'd get the money to buy the baking materials. He didn't think it was fair to use stuff from home. I looked at him closely as he said that. Either there had been talk at Paul's house about Mom and me not having much money to live on, or else Paul was really starting to think for himself.

Then Paul really surprised me. "Why don't we spend part of this weekend washing and de-fleaing people's dogs?" he suggested. "We could charge them enough to pay for the baking things, and for the Brewer's Yeast that we'd need. We could probably even work in our back yard. A lot of people walk by there with their dogs on a Saturday."

"What would you tell your mom?" I asked suspiciously. Too many things had been going wrong lately and our time was running out.

Paul smiled at me. "I'll tell her the truth." I started to protest, but he went on, "The truth is, we need to collect fleas because they have something to do with our science project for the science fair. Isn't that right?"

What he said was sort of close to the truth. Somehow, telling it that way made sense, although telling the truth doesn't always seem to work for me.

"Okay, we'll try it," I agreed. "Now, let's go talk to Mr. Thomas."

Surprisingly, Mr. Thomas agreed. "You two must be making a very interesting science project using fleas," he said. "I'm looking forward to seeing it."

I swallowed hard and glanced at Paul. He had a silly smile plastered on his face. Well, he'd told the truth. He said the fleas had something to do with the project. Mr. Thomas was the one who thought we were using them in the project. I waited for Paul to correct him, but he didn't.

I swallowed again and sighed. There was going to have to be a lot of explaining the day of the science fair. The truth couldn't be told then – for who would believe the truth anyway? No, we were going to have to work on making up an explanation that was credible enough for us to win first prize.

"You, Lisa, have actually been at the library doing research on fleas? Wonders never cease, do they?" Mr. Thomas joked. "Maybe there's hope for you yet in science."

It's a good thing Mr. Thomas is a good creative writing teacher, because at that moment my opinion of him as a science teacher was not very high.

"Yes, this afternoon you may do a demonstration on how to de-flea a dog and we will have the class start collecting them to study. Then if they wish, they may trade them to you for a recess treat." He chuckled. "You may never be scientists, but you'll probably make it big in the business world."

Paul was right. His mother didn't object to us washing dogs and de-fleaing them in the back yard once he explained that the fleas had "something to do with" our science project.

The next Saturday we made a sign and hung it on Paul's gate. The sign said:

NEEDED: FLEAS
FOR SCIENTIFIC RESEARCH
WE WILL DEFLEA AND WASH YOUR DOG
SAFELY, FOR $1.50

By figuring everything out, we knew we'd have enough to pay for everything if we did fifteen dogs. We hoped there were fifteen dogs with fleas in Paul's neighborhood.

Dog owners seemed to like the idea of contributing to "scientific research". They watched in awe as we sprinkled the Brewer's Yeast onto the animal's fur and fluffed it through with our hands. Then there were "Ohhhs" and "Ahhhs" and "Well, I nevers" uttered as little black fleas leapt out of the dog's fur and onto the white sheet – this time we'd asked for an old sheet– where we captured them and put them into Gagar's little bottle. There, they hopped around happily as if the jar did indeed contain some sort of magical nourishment.

Then we bathed each dog. Paul's mom had given us two bottles of shampoo she had planned on throwing out, and I soon knew why! Both of them smelled obnoxious. The only word to describe the odour of "green apple" or "cherry blossom" mixed with wet dog fur is VILE!

By three o'clock, we'd done seventeen dogs. We had twenty-five dollars and fifty cents in our pocket, and the bottle was nearly a quarter full of fleas.

When we saw Mrs. MacGillicuddy with her horrible little dog, Fifi, coming up Paul's street, we quickly took our sign down. Fifi's always scratching and she looks mangy, so I knew she was loaded with fleas. But I also knew she'd rather bite than smell like a cherry blossom. Besides, if I smelled one more "green apple" or "cherry blossom" dog, I was certain I'd throw up.

When I got home, Mom listened enthusiastically as I told her about our successful day. She was probably thankful I was finally putting some effort into science and hopeful my marks would improve as a result. She didn't have to worry. I knew my marks were going to improve because I was going to win that science fair with the golden grasshopper and the flying machine.

Through the window I watched a hawk gliding over the garden. I knew how that felt! Suddenly, I felt as if the golden grasshopper and I were up there with him. I closed my eyes and swayed a little dizzily as the ground rushed past me in a patchwork of colours, just as it had the other day.

When I was home alone, I'd gone on a flight all by myself. I'd swept over the whole farm, and gone higher than ever before until I could see the shimmering blue of Okanagan Lake and the cone shape of Mt. Boucherie to the east. Soft white clouds had once again beckoned me, and a shining rainbow glistened in the distance. Someday I would fly through a rainbow . . .

"By the way, Lisa, I'm going out to dinner and a show with Dr. Ferguson tonight," Mom said, bringing me back to earth with a jolt. I could tell by the look on her face she was waiting for my reaction. "I won't be late, and Mrs. Meyers from next door will be over shortly. Don't forget to do your homework and please stay out of mischief!"

I sighed. There was no use making a fuss. She would go anyway. Besides, I had other things to think about. "All right, Mom," was all I said.

I had an early supper and was up in my room thinking how I was going to spend my evening alone when Mom tapped on my door.

Ted had arrived and they were on their way, she told me as she stuck her head in the door and gave me a quick kiss. Then, almost as an afterthought, she opened the door wider and handed me a skirt and blouse.

"Auntie Teresa made this for you, dear," she said. She held it up in front of me. "My, she knows just what colour is right for you. It will look lovely on you. I hope you'll wear it Monday."

"Monday! You've got to be kidding!" I hated dresses. I'd never worn one to school.

"You'll hurt her feelings if you don't, honey. Besides, she's already started to make you a beautiful dress for the school dance after the science fair."

"School dance?" I squeaked. "But I'm not . . ."

"Of course you'll go, Lisa, especially if you win first prize. That's where they're going to present the award," she said. She looked at me and smiled. "Besides, you're getting to the age where you could look really pretty if you tried. You don't want to be a tomboy all your life."

With that, she was gone, and I was left holding the skirt and blouse. I swung around and glanced into the mirror. The turquoise in the skirt was my favourite colour. With a sigh I tossed it onto the bed. I would have to think about it. I might wear it on Monday to make everybody happy, but I wasn't going to try it on until then.

I waited, listening, until I was sure Mom and Dr. Ferguson were gone. Then I got the bottle of fleas from the closet where I'd hidden it. Mom would have a fit if she knew the fleas were in the house.

I looked at them closely. They didn't look quite as healthy and happy as before. I shook the jar gently. A couple of them didn't move. Something must have gone wrong with whatever was in the jar to keep them healthy. I chewed on a finger-nail and shook the jar again.

They were going to have to be kept nourished or I would lose them, and all of our work would be wasted. I put the jar on the dresser and paced around the room chewing on another fingernail. Then I had an idea.

"Ro – per," I called, opening my bedroom door. Roper came bounding up the stairs, through my door, and leapt up onto the bed, landing on top of my new skirt and blouse.

I waved my arms at him. "Get off there, silly. I may have to wear that Monday and I don't want it decorated with paw prints. Come here."

He came over to where I was standing and looked up at me with that smile on his face. The smile that had been there ever since we got rid of his fleas.

"Now, Roper," I began, "you've already been involved in some scientific experimentation in order to help us win the science fair. You're a good dog for going along with all that," I went on, "so I'm sure that you won't object to doing one more thing in the name of 'scientific research'."

I stroked his silky back a few times and then looking into his trusting eyes, I quickly grabbed the bottle, opened it, and carefully dumped all of the fleas onto Roper's back.

CHAPTER 12

The next morning I was up bright and early to get all the fleas off Roper and back into the bottle before Mom got up. I'm not sure what the look in his eyes was as he crawled out from under my bed. Perhaps it was humiliation. He hung his head and whimpered softly while I de-fleaed him.

"Come on, Roper, be a sport," I scolded him. "After this is over, I promise you'll never have fleas again." I patted his wet nose and his tongue slurped over my arm. I supposed I was forgiven, although I'm not so sure he realized that we were going to do the same thing every night for the next while.

I tiptoed downstairs so as not to wake Mom. I hadn't heard her come in the night before and I wondered what "early" meant to her.

It was still an hour and a half before milking time. I poured some Shreddies into a cereal bowl and slathered on some thick, fresh cream and lots of brown sugar. Roper was eyeing me, so I filled his dog dish with Shreddies and a bit of milk, too. While putting the milk back in the fridge, I noticed the eggs and sour cream that we'd bought yesterday for our baking.

Looking out the window, I ate my cereal. It was going to be a beautiful day. The sun was already casting a rosy glow onto the apple blossoms on our nearby apple tree, and the birds were singing their hearts out. Perfume from the lilac bush wafted through the screen door. It was really going to be too nice a day to spend in the house baking.

There was probably enough time to bake some cakes before Mom even got up. She had offered to help Paul and me today, but I would surprise her. Rummaging around in the drawer, I found the recipe of Paul's that we'd decided on. It's one of his favourites. It's called Never Fail Chocolate Cake.

I got all the ingredients we'd bought and lined them up on the counter: sour cream, eggs, flour, white sugar, cocoa, baking powder, salt, soda, vanilla, and cinnamon hearts.

The recipe didn't really call for cinnamon hearts, and Paul had created quite a scene in the grocery store when I bought them. He said you shouldn't muck about with a good recipe. But I told him a good cook is creative, and that some day this new recipe might make me famous.

I've never done much baking. I'd much sooner be outside with Roper, racing around the farm and climbing trees. But it wasn't such a bad job, I decided, mixing up the batter. I began to hum a tune.

Mom came into the kitchen just as the batter was being scraped into the pan. She didn't seem as happy as I'd expected her to be when she saw what was happening.

"What are those red lumps?" she asked, frowning at the batter in the cake pans.

"Cinnamon hearts," I told her. "We figured we'd be creative."

"Let's hope the kids appreciate your creativity," she said with a smile as she poured some cereal into a bowl for herself. "Did you follow the recipe carefully?"

"Mom, I can read. Yes, of course I followed the recipe carefully." Turning the oven timer on, I headed for the door. "I'm going out to milk. I can finish doing Pansy before the cakes are done."

Paul had planned to help me bake the rest, but he had come down with the flu and had to spend the weekend in bed. His mom phoned while I was out milking and said that she'd bake the other two cakes for us.

When I came in from the milking to take my

cakes out of the oven, I was glad she had offered to do the rest. My cakes didn't look . . . well, they didn't look quite like I'd expected they would. A cake's supposed to rise, isn't it? Mine hadn't. They were only about one centimetre high and they were riddled with little red tunnels where the cinnamon hearts had sunk to the bottom.

Thank heavens Mom never saw them. She was out milking, and I slathered on a thick coating of icing and had them in the fridge before she got in.

"What happened to them?" was Paul's first question on Monday morning as he peered in at the cakes in the box. Then his eyes slid upwards from the box to me and his mouth dropped open. "What happened to you?"

He took a step backwards with that dumb look still on his face. "You . . . you've got a dress on."

I knew my face was turning red. I set the box down with a thud on the table and glared at him. "It's not a dress, dough head. It's a skirt and blouse! Haven't you ever seen a skirt and blouse before?"

"Not on you!" Paul said as he kept staring at me. I looked past him at the kids coming in the door. I could see Michael's blond head as he hung up his knapsack.

Paul was still looking at me as though he were in shock. "It looks . . ."

"Never mind!" I whirled and ran out of the room, around the corner, and into the girls' washroom.

Angrily, I brushed away the tears and told myself it was stupid to be crying over a silly old skirt and blouse. I just wouldn't come out until school was over, I decided.

I pulled myself up on the sink counter and folded my hands in my lap. Five minutes passed. I yawned and stretched. Then I settled back against the mirror. Another five minutes passed. I began to swing my legs back and forth and count to see how many swings to a minute. Then I tried to multiply in my head to see how many swings I'd be making in an hour. How about in a day? What if I sat here all day and nobody cared? I stopped swinging my legs.

The class would be doing math now. How many questions would I have for homework? What if I had as many questions for math homework as my legs would swing to the hour? Maybe I should slip out the door and walk home. I jumped down off the counter and was about to sneak out when the door opened and Diane and Jenny walked in.

Diane and Jenny weren't my best friends. I

didn't have any best friends, really. I usually stayed away from the other girls in my class because all they ever talked about was boys and clothes and when they'd be allowed to wear makeup. But Diane and Jenny weren't totally like that. Sometimes I even had fun with them, like last year when they joined me in a mud fight against the boys at recess.

Now, they stood staring at me like Paul had. Only they had sense enough to recover faster than he had.

"Wow, you look nice," breathed Diane.

Jenny gasped. "I love your skirt! Where did you get it?"

I glared at them. "Mr. Thomas sent you in to get me, didn't he? Well I'm not coming out, so there!"

"Why not?" they both chimed together.

"'Cause I got this on, that's why," I said, waving at my skirt. "They'll all stare at me."

"So what!" Diane said. "The only reason they'll all stare is because you look so different. No one's ever seen you in a skirt before. But you look pretty!"

They were looking at me as if they meant it.

"I do?" I whispered.

"Yes, you do," they both chimed again.

"Look at yourself in the mirror," Jenny said,

and she pulled my arm around so that I stood facing the mirror.

Well, I certainly did look different. The blues and greens in the skirt seemed to make my eyes sparkle. My hair hung down my back in a neat braid that Mom had tied a blue ribbon in at the last moment. And the outfit itself – well, I had to admit, it was okay.

"Come on, Lisa," Diane's voice pleaded. "We've got to get back to class. Mr. Thomas will be mad if we don't hurry."

I started to protest, still unsure.

Jenny opened the door and started walking out. "Walk behind us. You'll be all right."

One thing I've got say about Mr. Thomas. He must have threatened the kids within an inch of their lives because when we walked in, everyone was working hard at math and no one dared look up.

It wasn't until I sat down and started my work that I glanced up to see Brad Summers staring at me. I stuck my tongue out at him. He quickly returned to his math.

A few minutes later Paul walked by and, without Mr. Thomas noticing, dropped a folded up note onto my desk. It read:

Don't forget we have to sell cake at recess. The kids have lots of fleas.

P.S. You look nice. That's what I was trying to tell you.

I looked up, but Paul was standing with his back towards me, talking to Mr. Thomas. Michael was standing next to them waiting. He looked at me. He didn't stare, he just looked. Then he smiled. I looked away quickly and never looked up again until the recess bell rang.

Paul's cakes did look a lot better than mine. They had risen to the top of the pan and each piece came out looking fluffy and yummy. Most of the kids from our class, and many from other classes who'd heard about the "cakes for fleas" trade, were lining up with various sized bottles containing fleas. I pushed my cakes to the back of the table.

Michael was the last one to get one of Paul's pieces of cake. As I handed it to him he whispered, "You look nice, Lisa."

I didn't know where to look, and for once, I didn't know what to say. Suddenly, I felt glad I'd worn the new outfit.

"Hurry up, will ya!" whined Worm Face. "I want my cake."

Michael moved away and I cut into my cakes. As soon as I lifted the first piece out I knew something was terribly wrong. Instead of being light and fluffy, it was heavy and doughy with big air holes through it. The cinnamon hearts had bled a sickly pink colour into the surrounding area.

I quickly shoved the piece at Worm Face and tried to grab his bottle of fleas, but he pushed my arm away.

"Just a minute. I gotta see if this cake is good enough to trade my fleas for." He wrinkled up his nose then bit the piece of cake in half and started chewing it.

As he chewed, his eyes opened wide and his mouth began to pucker. He began gagging and choking, and his face turned red. Then he opened his mouth and spit the cake all over me. I don't really think he meant to spit on me. Even Brad Summers isn't that nasty. It must have just tasted so awful that he didn't think.

But when it landed on my new skirt – the skirt that I'd just decided I was glad to be wearing – I didn't stop to think either! I grabbed the cake pan, turned it upside down, and dumped the remaining cake on top of Brad Summers's head.

With a howl of anger, he tackled me. We both flew backward, knocking over the table with the other cake and some of the bottles of fleas on it. Other kids madly scrambled to get out of the way as we twisted and rolled on the ground, covered in Never Fail Chocolate Cake and white frosting.

Paul disappeared into the school in a hurry. He must have thought I'd turned into a wimp just because I had a dress on and was scared I'd get hurt. But I knew that I could beat up on Worm Face no matter how I was dressed.

Unfortunately, I never had the chance. I had a handful of cake ready to mush into Brad Summers's face when two shiny black shoes appeared in front of my nose. I looked up . . . into the furious eyes of Mr. Thomas.

CHAPTER 13

"You put how much baking powder in your cakes?" Mom asked me as if she didn't believe what she'd heard the first time.

"Four tablespoons," I told her again.

"Four tablespoons! No wonder Brad Summers spit it out. It must have tasted dreadful."

I pulled open the drawer and retrieved the recipe. We looked at it together.

"There," I said, pointing to the baking powder in the list of required ingredients.

With her fingernail, Mom scratched away a blob of dried batter from the page. "It may have looked like a '4' to you Lisa, but it's really 1/4. And 'tsp.' is short for 'teaspoon', not 'tablespoon'. You put in sixteen times as much baking powder as you were supposed to." She looked me in the eye and sighed. "The next time you decide to bake, please let me help you."

"Oh, don't worry Mom. I don't have to bake anymore. Even the kids who didn't get any cake gave me their fleas. They said if it tasted as bad as it looked, they'd give me their fleas so that I wouldn't bake anymore."

I went back to washing my skirt and blouse. Mom had not been pleased to see my new outfit covered in Never Fail Chocolate Cake, white frosting and dirt. She told me that my punishment was to scrub it until all the stains and dirt came out. I had enough sense not to argue with her, even though I figured that Mr. Thomas's punishment of grounds clean up every lunch hour for two weeks with Brad Summers was enough.

I went outside to hang up the skirt and blouse. As I let the screen door go, Roper yelped beside me. He must have been moving too slowly to keep from getting his tail caught in the door.

Come to think of it, he wasn't moving very quickly these days. In fact, he wasn't doing a whole lot of moving at all. I watched as he walked slowly over to a tree to lie down in the shade.

He must not be feeling well, I thought to myself. It couldn't possibly be the fleas I was putting on him every night, could it? He was probably just feeling sorry for himself. I hadn't been spending much time with him lately. I sat down beside him for a few minutes and stroked his back.

Paul and I had done very well with our flea

collection. Between washing dogs and the bake sale, we had Gagar's bottle nearly full. In fact, the lid had begun to glow that morning when I collected them off of Roper and put them in the container, but when I checked later, the light had gone out again. We still had nearly a week before Gagar was to return. Surely we would have enough to keep the light glowing by then.

The science fair was this coming Friday. I wondered if Mom was going to go out with Dr. Ferguson again tonight. If she did, then I could get some more practise with the flying machine. Mrs. Meyers would be coming over again to "house sit" as Mom calls it, but she never pays any attention to what I'm doing. She just sits and knits until she falls asleep, allowing me to do pretty much what I want to.

Mom and Dr. Ferguson had been seeing quite a bit of each other over the past couple of weeks. I stopped stroking Roper for a minute and thought hard. The idea that Dr. Ferguson had been seeing Mom a lot didn't bother me as much anymore. I wondered why. Maybe I'd been too busy with the flying machine and hadn't had time to worry about them.

Paul and I had worked hard on the flying machine so that everything would run smoothly on the day of the fair. He had painted it a glossy red and it had white lettering on the bottom saying LISA'S FLYING MACHINE. Paul had stuck to his original decision of not flying in it. In fact, he wouldn't even try the golden grasshopper. I guess he's just afraid of flying. But he seemed keen on helping me win first prize at the fair.

We had discovered a small problem. Having me sit in the seat, stroking the golden grasshopper and thinking about flying was not enough to get the thing into the air. I had simply floated out of my seat and up into the air until my hand, which was holding onto the crank for the propeller, could reach no more.

After that, we attached straps to the platform for my feet to slip under, and a belt which fastened me to the seat. That worked. I was now able to rise smoothly into the air, taking the flying machine with me. We had practised enough that we thought students and judges alike would be satisfied we had produced an authentic flying machine.

We were still working on an explanation for it. Paul thought we should tell them the truth – that a "being" from outer space had given us the ability to fly, but only for a short while. But I didn't want to tell the truth. I was pretty sure that no one would believe it anyway. And I didn't want to take the chance of anyone finding out about the flea capacitor. That was Paul's and my secret forever.

I decided that we should put a bottle of fleas on board and say that we didn't really know why it worked. We'd just discovered that it did. I mean, that's what science is all about, isn't it? Discovering things that work for some reason and then trying to figure out why.

Paul just shrugged his shoulders when I said that. I guess he figured that sounded more realistic than what was really true. We still had a few more days to decide on our final story.

I left Roper still lying under the tree. He looked up at me and thumped his tail on the ground. He had just been feeling sorry for himself, I decided, as I ran back to the house to phone Paul.

O O O

Although I'd die before admitting it to anyone, on Wednesday at school, during silent reading, I realized I was in love with Michael Black!

I'd been in the same class as Michael since kindergarten, and in grade three I'd even hit him over the head with the plastic base mat when we'd both wanted to play third base. He'd always been just one of the guys – like me – until last Monday. Until I'd worn that skirt and blouse.

Until he'd looked at me and smiled and told me I looked nice.

Since Monday, I couldn't seem to talk to Michael anymore, or even look at him. And when I thought he was looking my way, I started to feel warm all over. It's funny how just wearing a silly old skirt and blouse could make a person feel so different. But the feeling was wonderful.

I stared at the book in front of me for a long time before realizing the words weren't making any sense. I was still thinking about Michael. Finally, with a sigh, I reached inside my desk and, while pretending to read, I wrote this note:

Dear Michael

I love you. Do you love me too?

I started to sign my name and then stopped. I just couldn't do it. Looking around the room, I realized there were two other girls whose name began with an 'L': Lydia Smith and Linda Travis. He would know that the note was from one of us if I left the 'L'. That would be close enough.

I carefully folded it up into a little square and sat chewing my fingernail. Michael's blond head was bent over a book at his desk near the pencil sharpener. I'd drop it behind his desk and then kick it under as I walked by.

I got up from my desk on the pretence of having to sharpen my pencil, but when I passed Michael's desk, the note didn't get dropped. Between my desk and his, I had chickened out. I headed for the garbage can and opened my hand. I couldn't believe my eyes. It was gone! I whirled around and looked back.

Mr. Thomas was stooping over to pick it up from the aisle where I had dropped it. I watched in horror as he carefully unfolded it and announced to the class that he had a note to read to them.

CHAPTER 14

"How's your science project coming?" Michael asked me at recess. He had followed me out to the swings and now sat in the one beside me.

I kicked at the dirt with my toe, afraid to look over at him. I wondered if he knew that the note had been from me. It's Mr. Thomas's policy to read out loud every note that he catches. He must think that will stop the kids from writing them. The one good thing about it is that he never reads the signatures out loud.

He had given the note to Michael, much to my dismay. I prayed that he wouldn't ask me if I'd written it.

"My science project?" I asked dumbly. My mind took a moment to focus. I thought about my nightly excursions on the flying machine. "Oh, it's coming along fine . . . I guess. I'm nearly finished."

Now I did look at Michael. I was pretty sure that his project, whatever it was, wouldn't beat our flying machine. But he is smart – in fact he always gets straight A's on his report card. I wondered what he'd done for his project.

"How's yours coming?" I asked, hoping that he'd give me some clue.

"Pretty good," he replied with a sigh. "But I can't believe how much work it's been. You should see the research I've done, and the letters that I've written, and the time I've spent, putting it all together." He pushed himself off and swung past me. As he came back towards me, he looked at me and laughed. "I've sure learned a lot. I just hope that I can get it finished tomorrow night."

We swung back and forth beside each other for a few minutes. I started to push hard with my legs, until I zoomed past Michael. I didn't feel like talking any more. All of a sudden I felt unhappy.

The cool wind hit me in the face as I came down, then tugged at the back of my hair as I went back up. It was as if I were on the flying machine with the golden grasshopper. That should have made me happy, but it didn't. Why was I feeling this way?

Then it struck me. I was feeling guilty! Guilty about the probability of taking first prize at the science fair by cheating, when Michael had worked so hard on his project.

"There's the bell," Michael called as he jumped off his swing at the end of its arc. He waited as I slowed down by dragging my feet on the ground. I leapt off a little higher than I'd planned and landed on my knees in the sawdust beside him. I got up slowly and carefully brushed all the sawdust off my pants. I didn't look at him.

"You're coming to the dance on Friday, aren't you?" Michael asked as we walked back to the school.

I nodded my head.

"Will you dance with me, then?" he asked, not looking at me.

I nodded again without speaking. A little while ago, that would have caused me to die of excitement. But now, thoughts of the science fair were bothering me, and I barely felt anything.

"Good. See ya later," he said as he broke into a run to get into line with the other boys.

I walked slowly to the line-up, deep in thought.

CHAPTER 15

"What do you mean, you think the flea capacitor is getting weak?" Paul asked as we picked up the flying machine. "Gagar told us that the golden grasshopper would last until he got back."

"Yeah, but don't forget we've been using it a lot, and also, it's had this extra weight to lift," I said as we carried the flying machine through the trees behind the barn.

It was Thursday night and this was to be our last practise run. Dr. Ferguson had come over for supper and now he and Mom were having coffee. Paul and I had decided we would practise out by the pond where the trees would hide us, in case they happened to walk outside.

Dr. Ferguson had been giving Mom advice on running the farm more profitably. They'd spent quite a bit of time discussing possible changes. I was surprised that he hadn't tried to talk her into selling it, as Paul's father had after my dad left.

Dr. Ferguson was also encouraging my mom to go back to university for the degree she'd started before she'd married my dad. He'd offered her a part time job with enough pay so that she could afford to go. Maybe that wasn't such a bad idea.

Paul's voice broke into my thoughts. "This ought to be a good place." I looked around. You couldn't see the house or any part of the yard because of the trees.

"Yeah, it's good enough," I answered as we set the flying machine down and I climbed aboard.

I sat down, carefully slid my feet in under the straps and adjusted the belt which held me to the flying machine. I took the golden grasshopper out of my pocket, stroked its back gently and concentrated. My body strained against the straps, making the plywood platform creak. Slowly, we lifted off into the air.

"It looks fine to me," I heard Paul holler. I had to make him believe the golden grasshopper was weak if my secret plan was to succeed. When I looked down at him, I let my concentration waver for a second and the flying machine bounced around, as if it had a spluttering engine.

"See, it *is* getting weak," I shouted down. Paul shrugged. I wasn't sure if he believed me or not. I climbed a bit higher, and I wished it to go first left then right.

I was gliding over a small field, between two groves of trees. This field, according to Dr. Ferguson, should be ploughed up next spring and planted with a money making crop. He suggested herbs. It could be irrigated by water from the large pond beyond it.

I headed over to the pond and turned my thoughts to what must happen next. I had to concentrate to make sure everything would work according to plan.

I looked for Paul. He was running quite far behind, trying to catch up. I accelerated to a spot over the middle of the pond.

From above, the dark green water appeared deep and menacing. It seemed a long way down. My heart started thudding. Then I took a deep breath and reminded myself that I was a good swimmer. I would be all right, as long as the flying machine fell first.

When I unbuckled the waist strap the flying machine tugged at my feet as it started to fall. Quickly, I pulled both feet from under their straps.

As I hung safely suspended in the air by the golden grasshopper, the flying machine spiralled wildly down to the pond. But I had to make it appear as if I had gone down with it. I threw the golden grasshopper as hard as I could towards shore. It landed on the bank, glowing in the late afternoon sun.

Paul was running along the path to the pond. I shrieked loudly, hoping he would hear me, as I plummeted down into the water behind the flying machine.

When I surfaced, pieces of the shattered flying machine were floating all around me. With a "glurb", the propeller rose from the depths and sailed by. A flock of ducks, interrupted in their peaceful afternoon paddle, stretched their necks to fly squawking to safety.

Paul was still nowhere in sight. I swam quickly to shore and grabbed the golden grasshopper before he ran up, gasping and panting, his eyes wide with fear.

"I'm all right," I assured him before he could get a word out. I held out my hand with the golden grasshopper. "I told you it was getting weak," I said. I pulled a piece of pond weed out of my hair and shivered. "So much for the trip to Vancouver and bringing up my science mark."

"And so much for winning the science fair!" Paul said, squinting up at me. "I think you did this on purpose. I think you decided not to win the science fair, and so you ditched the flying machine into the pond."

I gasped and made a face. "I did not! Do you

think I want to go to summer school? Do you think I'm crazy?"

Paul regarded me closely. "Yeah, you usually are crazy. But this time I think you decided that cheating like this was wrong. I don't know what happened on Wednesday, but you've been sort of different since then."

I thought back to Wednesday and my talk with Michael. It was true. After hearing him say how much work he'd put into his project, I knew that what we were doing was really wrong, and we couldn't go through with it. But I hadn't wanted to let Paul know that I was turning soft. That's when I'd decided to sabotage the flying machine.

"I'm freezing," I told Paul as I headed back towards the house.

"You could have just told me, you know," Paul muttered as he tripped along behind me. "You didn't have to almost drown yourself just so I wouldn't know what you were doing. Bet that old grasshopper still works, doesn't it?" But I didn't answer. I just held the golden grasshopper tightly in my hand and kept walking towards the house.

"What happened?" Mom's voice was full of concern as she eyed my dripping clothes.

I glanced at Paul. "I was doing something stupid and I fell in the pond. I'm okay. I'm going up to change."

"Lisa . . ." Mom had followed me to the bottom of the steps. "Ted was out looking for you. He'd like to talk to you because Roper seems quite ill."

I changed in a hurry. Then I tore downstairs to the porch where Roper was lying in his basket.

He looked up at me mournfully. There was no thumping tail or slurping tongue. But his nose was wet and I knew that was a good sign. I squatted beside him and stroked his head.

When Dr. Ferguson came out, I jumped up to face him.

"Is he really bad? How sick is he? Is he going to die?" The words tumbled out of my mouth before Dr. Ferguson could say anything.

He frowned. "Well, he'll live, I think. It's not a matter of his being really sick, he's just terribly run down." He bent down to part the fur in various places on Roper's body. "There's something I just don't understand. His body is absolutely covered with flea bites, but I could only find a couple of fleas."

I gulped. "Is that why he's so run down?"

"Yes, it is," Dr. Ferguson replied. "It looks like he's had a regular army of them feeding on him."

I felt a tear slide down my face. "That's exactly what he's had," I cried as I threw my arms around Roper's neck and started sobbing.

Dr. Ferguson let me cry for a few minutes,

then he gently pulled me up. "Lisa, Roper's going to be okay. I've given him a good shot of vitamins. We'll keep a close eye on him for a few days and we'll make sure that no more fleas get on him." He turned me around to face him as he sat down on a bench. "Now, are you ready to tell me about it?"

I told him about the fleas and about how I'd been putting them on Roper every night for the last couple of weeks so they'd stay healthy. I didn't, of course, tell him about Gagar, and the real reason we needed the fleas. As I told the story I kept expecting him to get mad and to tell me what a stupid thing I'd done. But he waited patiently until I was finished. Only then did he begin to chuckle.

"Well, it's not a pretty story as far as Roper's concerned, but I'll bet no other bunch of fleas has ever been so well taken care of. They must be fat and healthy!" He laughed again. "I'm not so sure your mother should hear about this, Lisa. She may not think it's as funny as I do."

When Mom came out the screen door, I could tell by her face that she'd heard my story and that Dr. Ferguson was right. She didn't think it was very funny.

"Where are the fleas now, Lisa?" she demanded just as Paul walked out behind her.

I gave him a quick glance.

"Up in my room," I said quietly.

"Up in your room!" she shrieked. "Go and get them immediately and get rid of them. Don't ever bring fleas into this house again!"

○　○　○

"You have to!" I hissed to Paul up in my room.

"No way!" Paul hissed back. "My mother would kill me if she ever found out I had a bottle full of fleas in the house."

"Come on," I pleaded. "Gagar will be back for them the day after tomorrow. Just hide them so she doesn't see them."

Paul sighed and took the bottle from me, shoving it in his jeans pocket. "I gotta get going. It's almost dark." He turned to look back as he was leaving. "If I get into trouble because of you again, I'll . . . I'll . . ."

"You won't," I told him calmly as I followed him down the stairs. It's a good thing he didn't see me crossing my fingers behind my back.

CHAPTER 16

That night I had a weird dream that Gagar returned. Well, maybe it wasn't a dream. I'm not sure.

I had gone to bed early – all on my own. I was exhausted! Too many things had happened that day and my feelings were all jumbled up. Giving up winning the science fair had been a hard decision. Although I was glad I'd done the right thing, I still had a sick feeling in the pit of my stomach. And Roper . . . how could I not have realized he was getting sick?

In the middle of the night, I heard something scratching at my bedroom window. I sat up groggily. I wasn't really frightened. I think I sensed that Gagar had returned. When the silhouette of his enormous head and funny little body appeared through the screen on my window I could see the coloured lights racing around his belt. Gagar was still having trouble with his translator box. Every few seconds the lights would blink as he tried to speak.

"You're early!" I gasped. "You weren't supposed to come back until the day after tomorrow. The fleas are . . ."

The coloured lights raced in circles around the shadow of Gagar's waist. "The fleas . . ." he suddenly blurted out in the musical monotone voice I remembered. "What happened to the fleas?"

"We've got them. We have the jar full. It glows red. They're with Paul. He had to take them home," I explained.

The coloured lights went out and I saw Gagar whack the box several times. They flashed back on dimly, and in a voice that was clearly running out of power, it moaned slowly, "The fleas . . . the fleas . . ." Then the lights went out for good. I could tell that Gagar was trying to coax more power from the box because he still wanted to talk to me. But after a few minutes he threw up his hands in despair. I blinked and looked again. His silhouette was gone.

I climbed out of bed and went to the window. Trees rustled in the wind outside my window, but I couldn't see anything. I crawled back into bed and closed my eyes.

When I awoke again my alarm clock said 3:45 a.m.. I ran to the window for another look. The moon had risen and eerie shadows danced over the silvery ground as tree branches swayed in the wind. Neither Gagar nor his spaceship were anywhere to be seen. Had I dreamt it or imagined it? Or had it really happened? What had he meant when he asked, "What happened to the fleas?"

Back in bed, I tossed and turned for a long time before I could go to sleep again.

CHAPTER 17

Friday – science fair day – and Paul wasn't at school. What could have happened to him? The science projects were all on display in the gym, and after school I went in to have a look. They hadn't been judged yet, but it was obvious that everyone had put a great deal of effort into the projects.

Michael's, though, was the most impressive. He had collected leaves from the trees in our area and had laminated them onto cards. He'd done a write-up on each leaf, and he'd made a classification system for them on a big wall chart. As I looked at it, I knew that he'd told the truth when he said he'd done piles of work.

When I got home, I spent some time with Roper before supper. He'd begun to perk up already. He was still thin, and his coat wasn't shiny like it used to be, but he thumped his tail when he saw me and smiled.

The phone rang while I was out petting Roper. It was Paul. He wanted to know who'd won the science fair. I told him that I didn't know, that the judging was to be done before the seven o'clock dance. It was five-thirty now.

"Are you coming tonight?" I asked. "Where were you today? Why weren't you at school?"

"I was at home. I . . . ." I could hear Auntie Teresa in the background. "I gotta go. I'll see you at the dance." And he hung up before I could ask any more questions.

Mom had made lasagna for supper. It's usually one of my favourite foods, but I just didn't feel like eating. I guess I was too excited. I ate a few mouthfuls to please her and then excused myself to get ready.

After I had my bath, I put on the dress that Auntie Teresa had brought me. It was made of a silvery white shiny material and it had a full skirt. Around the neck was a long piece of the material to make a bow. I twirled around a few times in front of the mirror. I looked all right.

I took the gold chain that my grandmother had given me for Christmas out of my drawer. I hadn't worn it very many times because I'd never dressed up much before now. I undid the clasp to slide the medallion off. It was nice, but tonight belonged to the golden grasshopper.

I took it out and looped the chain tightly around its head. Then I put the chain around my neck and tucked the golden grasshopper inside the bow so that Mom wouldn't notice it.

Mom did my hair downstairs. She blew it dry and then she gathered a bunch of curls to the top of my head while the rest fell down my back. It felt strange to have a floating mass of hair behind me instead of braids flopping around. Different, but nice.

Dr. Ferguson arrived just as Mom finished with my hair. "My, aren't I lucky to be escorting two beautiful ladies to the dance." He smiled as he walked over to kiss Mom on the cheek. She did look pretty. "I hope you'll save one dance for me, young lady," he said, looking my way.

"Me?" I said laughing. "I don't know how to dance . . ."

The gym was full of people milling about when we arrived. I strained my neck and could see the first place ribbon on Michael's project. Mr. Thomas approached us.

"Good evening," he said, nodding to Mom and Dr. Ferguson. He smiled at me. "Why Lisa . . ." he began, then stopped. He probably wanted to comment on my appearance, and then remembered what had happened on Monday when I had worn my skirt and blouse for the first time.

He cleared his throat. "I'm sorry to hear about the fleas. That was an unfortunate accident to have happen the night before the science fair. However, I'm still willing to take into consideration the fact that you were working on a project."

"The fleas?" I echoed in a hollow voice. "What fleas?"

Mr. Thomas looked at me strangely. "Your fleas. The ones you were using in your science project. The ones that got loose in Paul's house last night."

My mouth made an O shape. Just then I saw Paul. He was a mess! His face and hands were all red and splotchy and puffy from scratching. An oily, white ointment covered his face.

I quickly excused myself and rushed over to him with Mom and Dr. Ferguson close behind.

"What happened to you?" Mom asked Paul in dismay.

Paul rarely tells fibs. He looked up at Mom. "I took the bottle of fleas home with me last night. The lid on the bottle must have come loose while I was riding my bike. I didn't want Mom to see them, so I stuck them under my pillow." Paul stopped and looked at me. "They all got loose in the night and bit me." He put his hand up to scratch at his face.

Mom grabbed his hand and pulled it away from his face. "Don't scratch. It'll only make it worse." She seemed about to hug him, but had second thoughts on looking at the gooey cream on his face.

"Where's your mom?" she asked Paul.

"She wanted to come, but she decided she'd better have the house fumigated. She thinks they're all over."

I could feel Mom's eyes boring into me. I looked at her with a sick smile on my face. She didn't smile back.

"*Lisa* . . ." I could tell from the tone of her voice that there was more to come. I spotted Michael waving at me from the other side of the gym.

"Aw, Mom, can't we talk about it later? Look, there's Michael. I want to go over and congratulate him." I smiled my sweetest smile at her as I backed away. I half expected her to call me back, but she didn't. I knew that I was in for it later, though.

Dr. Ferguson winked at me with an amused look on his face. Was he thinking the same thing I was? How did Paul taste to the fleas after they had dined on Roper all week? I stifled a giggle.

"I'm sorry about your face. I'll talk to you later," I whispered to Paul as I headed over to Michael.

The music blared out all at once. The grownups winced. It was quickly turned down to a less deafening roar. I congratulated Michael on winning.

"It's too bad your project didn't turn out," Michael said. "I guess you're disappointed."

I thought about the trip to Vancouver and the visit to the Planetarium. I thought about my low science mark and the probability of having a tutor over the summer and being stuck in the house to study.

"Yeah, I guess I am a little disappointed." Then I thought about Michael and how hard he'd worked on his project. "But it's probably for the best," I added.

Mr. Thomas had said he would still take into consideration the fact that I was working on a project. Maybe . . . just maybe if I worked hard and didn't daydream anymore in class . . .

We stood in silence for a few minutes, not sure what to do. Then, all of a sudden, he grabbed my arm and pulled me out onto the dance floor.

"Want to dance?" he asked when we were both standing on the dance floor facing each other. I laughed. It was good to know that he was nervous, too.

We stood there and moved our feet back and forth to the beat through two songs. When a slow song started, I noticed Brad Summers over by the light switches.

Suddenly, the gym was plunged into darkness. A few seconds later, when the lights all came on again, Mr. Thomas was over talking to Brad. Then all the lights dimmed to leave us in a sort of twilight zone.

Michael looked at me. "You want to try a slow one?" he asked.

I glanced over to where Mom and Dr. Ferguson were dancing. It didn't look too hard. Then I looked again. They were dancing awfully close together. Funny though, it didn't bother me anymore. In fact, it gave me kind of a warm feeling all over to see them together like that. I looked back to Michael.

"Sure," I said.

Michael put his hands on my waist and I put mine on his shoulders the way most of the other girls were doing. We shuffled back and forth to the music. Another two lights were turned off. I closed my eyes and swayed to the music, aware that Michael's face was very close to mine.

What would it be like to kiss him? I opened one eye and looked at him. It was hard to tell because of the light, but it appeared as if his eyes were closed, too. I puckered my lips up. Is this the way it was done? I leaned slowly, slowly forward.

My lips suddenly made contact with something that didn't feel anything like a mouth. I opened my eyes and found myself staring into his left ear.

Michael quickly turned and looked at me. "I'm sorry," I apologized. "I must have tripped. It's so hard to see."

Michael laughed. "That's okay." He looked at my neck. "What's that on your necklace? It's awesome."

I held it up for him to have a better look. "Oh this? It's a grasshopper . . . a golden grasshopper." Michael put his finger up and stroked its back.

For a second I felt weightless, as if I were going to float up through the roof of the gym and into the night sky, taking Michael with me. I looked out the open door into a velvet sky full of crystal stars. One in particular seemed to wink at me as it glowed brightly with a strange reddish light.

As I stared at it, a perfect image of Gagar drifted into my mind. His enormous black eyes bore into mine and the coloured lights raced around his belt as he sent me a message. He understood about the fleas. This time I knew it was no dream.

I gently dropped the golden grasshopper back inside the folds of my bow. "Yeah, it *is* neat," I said to Michael. I thought of the few precious flights that were left in the golden grasshopper and wondered if, just maybe, Gagar would come back and visit us again and give us another chance.

As the music stopped and the lights came on, I noticed Paul standing forlornly by himself against the wall, scratching at his face again. He was probably feeling guilty because all our fleas got away, and he was probably upset because his mom was mad at him. I decided I'd better go and ask him to dance, even if he was all flea-bitten. I owed him that much.

Besides, I wanted to tell him a couple of things. I wanted to tell him that I was glad I had made the decision I had about the flying machine and that it didn't really matter about the fleas getting away. I'd also better tell him that I'd be over tomorrow to see his mother and tell her it was my fault that Paul had the fleas in their house.

"Hey, you want to go hiking on Sunday, Lisa?" Michael asked as we walked towards Paul. "We could ride our bikes down to the creek. Let's ask Paul if he wants to come."

I grinned at Michael. "Sure," I said easily.

Rosemary Nelson was born in the small town of Dinsmore, Saskatchewan. Living in the wide open spaces with neighbourhood children few and far between, her imagination became her best friend.

Today, Rosemary is a teacher-librarian. She lives with her husband in British Columbia's Okanagan Valley. They have a beautiful acreage overlooking the lake and valley where they raise alpaca.

The Golden Grasshopper is Rosemary's second book with Napoleon, the first being *Dragon in the Clouds,* published in 1994.